HATING TO Love YOU

ERIN RYLIE

Hating to Love You
Copyright © 2019 by Erin Rylie
www.erinryliewrites.com

Editor: Erica Russikoff of Erica Edits
Interior Formatting: Brooke Cumberland
Cover Design: Jay Aheer, Simply Defined Art

All rights reserved. Without limiting the rights under copyright reserved above, no part of this publication may be reproduced, stored in, or introduced into a retrieval system, or transmitted in any form or by any means (mechanical, electronic, photocopying, recording, or otherwise) without the prior written permission of both the copyright owner and the above publisher of the book. This is a work of fiction. Any references to historical events, real people, or real places are used fictitiously. Other names, characters, places, and events are products of the author's imagination, and any resemblance to actual events or places or persons, living or dead, is entirely coincidental.

For my Nerds — without you ladies, none of this would be even remotely possible.

CHAPTER ONE

WELL, tonight is a complete shitshow, Rafe thought blandly as he watched his third public intoxication call of the night relieve himself on the brick wall outside the bar. Hearing a snort of laughter, he turned to look at his partner, Ramirez, who was clearly enjoying *his* evening.

"Should we let 'ol boy finish?" Ramirez stage-whispered, jerking his head at the drunk idiot.

Rafe shook his head at his partner, a rueful smile tipping up the corners of his lips. Pulling his flashlight from his belt, he shined the bright light into the drunk's face. "HPD, we're going to need you to wrap it up, sir."

The pisser, as he would henceforth be known, jerked and looked up at Rafe. Instead of immediately straightening and tucking his dick back into his pants, the moron turned, raising his hands. At the telltale sound of liquid hitting leather, Rafe looked down at his shoes. The fucking idiot was *still peeing*. On. Rafe's. Boots.

Ramirez couldn't hold it in any longer; he doubled over, boisterous laugh booming. As the pisser's stream of urine finally tapered off, he shot Rafe a lopsided grin. "S'alright, Officer. Bathroom inside's taken. I don' mind peein' out here."

"Well kid, unfortunately for you, the owner of this fine establishment happens to mind very much. Zip up your pants, put your hands against the wall, and spread 'em."

As Ramirez cuffed the pisser and read him his rights, Rafe stepped into the bar and headed toward the bathroom, intent on at least rinsing his boots off. They were starting to smell.

Fantastic.

Focused on walking through the narrow tables in the bar's seating area, he failed to notice the intoxicated group of women getting up from their table. Before he could change course, one of them looked up and spotted him.

"Oh em gee. Are you the stripper?" she asked in an excited voice. She was wearing a tiny white dress, a "bride" tiara topping her long, blonde curls.

"Excuse me?" he grated. He was not in the mood for this. He just wanted to wash his boots, drop the pisser off at the station, and get his paperwork done so he could go home.

The blonde, clearly not sensing his tone, was squealing and thanking her friends. "I can't believe you got me a hot cop stripper! Best bachelorette party ever!" Turning back to face Rafe, she put her hands on his chest, looked up at him, and practically purred, "How about we get these clothes off of you?"

"Ma'am," he started, plucking her perfectly manicured hands from his chest, "I'm an actual Houston Police Department officer. Please step back."

Her eyes widened, and she backed up, gracelessly plopping her ass back into her chair. "How is that possible? Look at you! You just *look* like a stripper," she exclaimed.

"As...flattering as that is, I'm an HPD officer. Now, if you'll excuse me."

"Wait!" she yelled, jumping up once more. "Please at least take a picture with me. I won't take no for an answer."

Knowing it would be quicker if he just agreed to take the damn picture, he nodded. She wrapped her hands around his bicep and cocked her hip, smiling at the camera. Rafe forced his lips into some semblance of a smile and tried not to wince when the bright flash went off in the dark bar.

"Have a good night, ma'am," he said, already walking away. After rinsing his boots off, he hauled ass back outside, making sure to take a different path through the tables in an effort to avoid the bachelorette party.

Thankfully, Ramirez and the pisser were comfortably settled in the police cruiser. He dropped into the driver's seat, turned off the light bar on top of the car, and pulled out onto Richmond Avenue. About a mile into the drive, Ramirez started making sniffing noises, rotating his head in a semicircle as though looking for the source of a smell.

"Hey pretty boy," Ramirez said, referring to him by the nickname most of the force had taken to calling him after he'd gotten asked out by a suspect on his first patrol out of the academy. "Do you smell something?"

Rafe shot him a puzzled look. "Umm, no?"

"Huh, I could've sworn I smelled piss. Where could that possibly be coming from?"

"Oh fuck off, dude. You better not tell anyone about this."

"Oh...so I shouldn't have sent out a mass text about it?"

Shitshow indeed. Rafe would never live tonight down.

The next morning, Rafe was up at seven o'clock sharp. He'd finally gotten home around three in the morning and had barely stripped off his clothes before hitting the bed and passing out. Rubbing a hand down his face, he stumbled into the bathroom and turned on the shower. He and Ramirez had been on the late shift for over a month now, but his sleep schedule hadn't evened out. No matter how late he got home, he was up by seven every single morning.

After a quick shower, he downed a bottle of water, grabbed his keys, and started his mile jog to the gym. When he checked in at the counter six minutes later, the woman manning the desk gave him a strange look before turning beet red. He brushed it off as nothing until it happened again when he was doing lunges. And again during his cool down session on the treadmill.

What the hell is going on?

His workout completed, he headed back home, stopping at the coffee shop by his apartment for his usual cup of black coffee. As he stepped out of the humid Houston air and into the coffee shop, Tiffany, the barista, giggled and blushed before turning around to prepare his drink.

"Good morning, Tiffany," he said, determined to get to the bottom of this mystery. "Is everything alright?"

"Hey Rafe!" she replied, far too brightly. "Everything's great, why?"

"I've been coming here for a year, and you've never giggled or blushed when I walked in the door."

"Oh. That. Um, well..." she started hesitantly. "I guess I just can't believe I serve coffee every morning to 'Houston's Hot Cop.'"

"What are you talking about?" he asked, dread settling low in his stomach.

"You're an Instagram sensation!" She pulled out her phone, opening the Instagram app before handing him the device. There on Instagram, with over a million likes, was his picture. The one from last night. The caption read, "Ladies, I've found him—the hottest cop in Texas! The best part? No wedding ring!"

"This is a joke, right? I mean this has to be a joke. Shit like this doesn't happen in real life," he asked rhetorically.

"Well, I mean you are pretty hot, Rafe. You know, blonde hair, blue eyes. You've got surfer boy written all over you."

"Great, that's just great." Rafe left the coffee shop, feeling the sudden urge to keep his head down as he walked home. Climbing the steps to his apartment building, he hoped his co-workers hadn't seen the picture. Not a lot of the guys on the force were into Instagram, thankfully, but plenty of the girls were.

Maybe it isn't that big a deal.

He let himself into his apartment, bending down to rub his orange tabby, Socks, behind the ears before setting his keys down on the small end table next to the door. He hesitated for a moment before picking up his phone, dreading the possibilities. Before he could even press the home button to unlock it, he got a text notification. As the text lit up his screen, he took in the other messages waiting for him. All fifty of them. And not just texts. Facebook notifications and emails cluttered his screen—all from friends, family, and news stations. Seriously. News stations. How was a stupid picture news?

After a few minutes of going through texts, mostly from his fellow officers, his stomach dropped at the curt message from his captain.

Captain Stevens: Get to my office by 10 a.m. Plain clothes.

Shit. Glancing at the time on his phone, Rafe realized he had an hour to get down to the station. He hopped in the shower, washing away the sweat and grime from his workout, and changed into a Henley and some jeans.

No more than thirty minutes after receiving the text, he was walking through the front doors of the station. He rushed through the desks in roll call, keeping his head down. Maybe if he didn't meet his co-workers' eyes, they wouldn't say anything to him. He had almost made it to his captain's office—was only two steps away—when he heard the voice of his most obnoxious fellow officer.

Of course, Davis is here. Of fucking course.

"Look out, ladies! Houston's hottest cop just walked in, and word on the street is, he's single!" he said loudly, spreading his arms and walking toward Rafe with a shit-eating grin.

"Cut it out, man," Rafe growled through clenched teeth. "Today isn't the day to mess with me."

"Oh! I'm sorry, *Officer Pierce*. Do you have bachelorette parties you need to get to? Lap dances to give?"

Brent Davis had graduated from the police academy in the same class as him and could never accept that Rafe had graduated at the top of his class, while Davis graduated... well, not at the top. Davis was constantly making fun of Rafe. Never his job performance—that was untouchable; he was one of the best on the force. No, Davis went after his looks. As if Rafe could help the way he was born. As if teasing Rafe could change the fact that Davis was born with a wiry frame, which never could quite seem to bulk up, and a permanent sneer on his lips.

Just as he stepped up to Davis, intent on giving him an unforgettable tongue-lashing, Captain Stevens stepped out of his office.

"Davis, Pierce, knock it off. Rafe, in my office. Now."

Brent smirked at Rafe before sauntering back to his desk. Resisting the urge to punch the bastard in the back of his retreating head, he took a deep breath and turned around. His stomach began to plummet as he walked into the captain's office. Captain Stevens wasn't one to mince words, and Rafe had a feeling he was in for a thorough ass chewing.

Stevens didn't even wait until Rafe was seated before speaking. "Are you out of your damn mind? Do you want to tell me why the hell you were inside of a bar taking pictures with some woman while Ramirez was outside cuffing your suspect alone? Do you even understand the concept of *partnership*?"

Rafe knew better than to answer those questions. Now was not the time to bring up the pee on his boots; it was a flimsy excuse and he knew it. Instead he stayed silent, hoping the questions were rhetorical and the captain didn't actually expect an answer.

After a few tense moments of silence, Stevens continued, "Look, I know you're one of the best we've got, but I'd love nothing more than to suspend your ass for this. Lucky for you, the media is obsessed with this stupid 'Hot Cop' story. It's good publicity for the station, and we're going to capitalize on it."

Rafe didn't like the direction this was heading. Ramirez was the attention seeker in their duo. He'd flirted and winked at just about every female in Houston and would be eating this up. Rafe, however, had never liked the attention his looks got him. He was constantly made fun of by his friends, fellow classmates, and now co-workers. Women hit on him for all of the wrong reasons. They just wanted a trophy boyfriend; none of them actually searched for substance with him. He just wanted this whole mess to go away, and if the captain was hinting at what Rafe thought he was, things were about to get really damn rough.

"The *Houston Reporter* wants to do a piece on you. And you're going to let them. I want you to be the picture of cooperation. I don't want to hear a single complaint about you. If that reporter says *jump*, you better jump. Got it?"

Though he wanted to protest, he knew he was in a tough spot. If he didn't cooperate, the captain would suspend him. His work meant too much to him for that to happen. Maybe he could just channel Ramirez for a few weeks, pretend he was loving all of this attention. Knowing his life was about to become a living hell, Rafe said the only thing he could, "Yes, sir."

CHAPTER TWO

SOPHIE HATED PRETTY BOYS. A girl could only suffer so many heartbreaks before turning cynical. Her high school boyfriend, Shane, was devastatingly handsome—black hair, green eyes, and a gorgeous smile. A smile that had entranced her as a poor, innocent freshman. She dated him for two years before realizing that his smile had also "entranced" half of the girls in their class.

Her college sweetheart, Michael, was quarterback for the University of Texas football team, and a legend in his own right. With beautiful, tanned skin, killer dimples, and soft brown eyes, he had convinced her that her high school boyfriend was a fluke, that there were good and honest men in the world. He'd cheated on her with the kicker of his football team. He and his partner were now happily married with an adorable adopted baby girl.

Goodie for them, she thought bitterly.

Her fiancé, Charlie, was the straw that broke the camel's back. Though not classically handsome, he had a ruggedness to him that had definitely appealed to her. He'd been well over six feet tall and muscular, sporting a beard and luscious long hair that he tied into a man-bun on most days. They had been together for three years before she'd walked in on him screwing one of the waitresses from the restaurant where he worked as a head chef.

As if that wasn't bad enough, the smug prick hadn't even panicked at being caught. No, he kept thrusting and suggested a threesome. Sophie didn't know how she would erase the image of his perfectly sculpted ass clenching as he'd continued to pump into that damn waitress.

So, when her editor had asked her to do a series of features on "Houston's Hot Cop," Sophie had spent a good two hours vehemently protesting. To no avail. Here she sat, in a quaint little Montrose coffee shop, waiting for a man more handsome than any she'd ever seen. He honestly looked like a scruffy Hemsworth brother. She'd seen the picture on Instagram, and though he'd looked supremely uncomfortable, Officer Raphael Pierce was undeniably gorgeous.

This was going to be miserable. He'd probably saunter in here, acting like he hung the damn moon. No doubt he'd flirt with every woman in the coffee shop. The only thing keeping Sophie in her seat was the promise her editor-in-chief had made her: *"Write this feature—and I mean really write it, Soph; don't half ass it—and I'll personally write your recommendation letter."*

Since graduating college and moving back to Houston, Sophie had dreamed of working for Nottingham Publishing, one of the biggest publishing firms in the country. Unfortunately, publishing jobs were almost impossible to land unless you were looking to be a poorly paid intern or had connections. Saddled with too many student loans to count and no connections, she couldn't afford to follow her dream. She'd applied for every job in the city that even remotely involved writing or editing. Only the *Houston Reporter* had responded.

So, she wrote fluffy editorial pieces and acted as a copyeditor. For years she'd been working to prove herself to her boss—Karen Stanley. Well known in the industry, Karen's recommendation could get just about any person any job they wanted. Her recommendation letters were an aspiring writer or publisher's dream come true. The catch was, they came about as often as leap year.

Sophie sipped her chai tea latte and gave herself the best pep talk she could muster.

You've got this, just stay professional. Write some sappy article about how he really is a good guy underneath that pretty face, and get that recommendation letter from Karen.

Sighing, Sophie tried to buy her own pep talk, she really did, but she couldn't deny that she was dreading this. Sticking the tip of her thumb in her mouth, she began to chew on the nail, chipping off the pretty red nail polish her best friend had painstakingly coated her nails with. At the sound of a throat clearing, she looked up from the table and met the clear, blue gaze of the man of the hour himself.

Sophie's mouth watered, *actually freaking watered*, as she took him in. Longish dark blonde hair, shorter on the sides than on top, a perfectly symmetrical face with day-old scruff, and a muscular but lean body made him the perfect specimen of a man. As nonchalantly as possible, Sophie tucked her fist under her chin, resting it on the table. Without support, it was entirely possible her chin would drop and she would be officially gaping.

No man should look this good. He wasn't even dressed

up! He was wearing dark-wash jeans that showcased his muscular thighs (*yum*) and a simple, light blue Henley. Was she staring? She was pretty sure she was staring.

Say something, Soph. Open your mouth and say something! What can I say though? Hi, I'm Sophie and I'd like to climb you like a tree. No, now is not the time to channel my inner Melissa McCarthy. Just say hi. You can do it. Hi. One syllable.

He ran his hand through his hair and rubbed the back of his neck awkwardly, accentuating the bulging biceps hiding beneath the long-sleeved shirt. "Are you Sophie Klein?" he asked, his hesitant grin tipping up the corners of his mouth.

"Umm, yes?" she said, wincing when the words came out like a question. She cleared her throat, determined to at least sound confident. "Yes, I'm Sophie Klein from the *Houston Reporter*, thanks for agreeing to meet with me!" she exclaimed, pasting on her most enthusiastic smile and standing to shake his hand.

The moment their hands made contact, she swallowed a gasp. Electricity and heat zinged through her system, and she struggled to maintain her firm handshake as a swarm of butterflies took residence in her stomach. When she heard Raphael suck in a sharp breath, she looked up to meet his eyes. He maintained eye contact for a brief moment before his gaze dipped and he took in her appearance. After a leisurely perusal of her crisp white button-down, simple navy pencil skirt, and nude stilettos, his gaze met hers again. The heat in his eyes almost took her breath away.

So this is what insta-lust feels like. Holy shit.

He barked out a laugh just as she realized she'd said the words out loud. Moment over and cheeks heating, Sophie snatched her hand back, smoothed her skirt, and returned to her seat. Raphael took the seat across from her, wearing what could only be described as a self-satisfied smirk.

"I'm Rafe, by the way. You forgot to ask when you were practically throwing yourself at me a moment ago," he said, smirk growing into a full-fledged smile. Sophie fought the urge to scowl at him, instead forcing a smile to her lips.

"Right, well, should we get started, *Mr. Pierce*?" She pointedly emphasized his last name and pulled out her phone to begin recording their conversation. "I'll be recording our interview, if that's alright with you. We can start with some basic questions about your time as an officer, and then I'd like to learn more about how that picture was taken. Sound good?"

"That's all great, but my name is Rafe," he said, glancing around for a server.

"Mr. Pierce," she began again, waving at Julie, the sweet blonde waitress who took care of her every time she visited her favorite coffee shop in the area.

Before she could finish her sentence, Rafe fixed his cool blue gaze on her and said once more, "Rafe."

Narrowing her eyes, Sophie refused to give in. She'd already humiliated herself; the last thing she wanted to do was concede defeat in this. "*Mr. Pierce*," she replied determinedly.

Before he could respond, Julie blessedly walked up to take his order.

"Hey! What can I get ya?" she asked cheerfully. Julie was always so damn peppy. Sophie would swear the girl had been a cheerleader in high school. She was a young college student, studying business management. With blonde hair, gray eyes, and an athletic figure, she was classically beautiful.

Rafe shot Sophie a mischievous smile before turning to Julie. He stuck out his hand, a broad smile showing off those irresistible dimples, and introduced himself.

"Hi, I'm *Rafe*," he said, putting unnecessary importance on the nickname with a meaningful look at Sophie. Poor Julie didn't stand a chance—the man was turning the full force of his charm on her. "What's your name, doll?"

Julie blushed prettily and stuttered out her name before again asking what she could get them. Rafe ordered black coffee and Sophie just shook her head to indicate that she didn't need anything. As Julie walked away to get his drink, Sophie watched Rafe, waiting for him to turn to check out their waitress. Shockingly, he returned his gaze to her, the weight of it making her shift in her seat.

Sophie cleared her throat and looked down at her chai tea, focusing on the light foam at the top of the cup. Taking a moment to get her thoughts in order, she took a big sip of the delicious drink and returned the mug to its saucer before clearing her throat and hitting start on the recording app on her phone.

"Alright, Officer Pierce. Let's get started."

CHAPTER THREE

RAFE WAS BEING AN ASS. On his way to the coffee shop, he had run through his approach to this whole situation in his mind. He was convinced that the only way to get through this mess was to adopt Ramirez's approach to everything. His partner was cocky, obnoxious, and a total flirt. He tended to be a bit of a pig, honestly, calling all of the female witnesses "doll" or "sweetheart." Rafe was more straightforward, and he certainly wasn't a flirt.

When he'd walked in and spotted the reporter waiting for him, he'd done an immediate double take. The girl looked like a complete tight ass. She was scowling down at her drink like it had done something to offend her while chewing on one brightly painted nail. Her hair, straight and blonde, was pulled into a severe bun at the nape of her neck, making her features seem more severe.

Rafe hadn't been in the mood to deal with a grumpy pain-in-the-ass reporter. Though he would have loved nothing more than to walk out and forget this interview all together, he was more scared of the captain than he was of some tiny waif of a woman with a scowl on her face. He'd straightened his shoulders, adopted Ramirez's trademark smirk, and sauntered over to the table like he owned it.

He hadn't expected to feel the sizzle of a connection when she'd stood up to shake his hand, and he certainly hadn't expected the word *lust* to come out of that sexy bow of a mouth. The moment the word passed from her lips, his dick had actually twitched. Nothing could have stopped him from his slow perusal of her body. The skirt she was in did great things for her curves, and the beige fuck-me heels she was wearing? He was half hard by the time he had sat down. Arguing with her over his name had actually been fun, and he'd started to enjoy himself, until she'd pulled out her damn phone and began grilling him.

They'd already talked about his early career, and she was now delving into what made him want to be a cop. He'd never told anyone why he'd become an officer, always brushing off the question with a shrug. He wasn't about to tell her about his fucked-up childhood—his drug-addicted mother and absent father. The truth was, he wanted to be a cop because when his mom finally overdosed, the officers on the scene had been like heroes to him.

After ten years of never eating enough, wearing threadbare clothes, and receiving beatings from his mom's "boyfriends," those men and women had saved him. They'd taken him out of the run-down, dilapidated house he and his mother had lived in and placed him in the foster care system.

He had never been adopted, but it had been a stable life for him in a time when all he'd needed was stability. The officers who had found him had even checked in with Rafe throughout the years, making sure the foster care system was treating him well.

But there was no way in hell he was going to share that with the reporter in front of him. He needed to distract her, get her off of that question. So when she repeated the question, he said the douchiest thing that came to mind.

"Mr. Pierce, did you hear me? What made you want to work in law enforcement?"

He let out a short laugh and put on the most charming grin he could muster. "Doll, I became a cop for the same reason most young, horny men straight out of college become one. Ladies love a man in uniform." Then he threw in a wink for good measure.

Though she managed to turn her scoff into a light cough, she was unable to hide the roll of her eyes.

"Charming," she muttered. "Okay, tell me what happened last night at the bar. How did the woman on Instagram even get a picture of you in a bar while you were on duty?"

"Well, darlin'..." he said, adding as much condescension to the word as he could. "My partner, Ramirez, and I got called to the bar for a public intoxication complaint. The idiot kid was so hammered that he was pissing on the wall of the bar when we pulled up. When I shined a light in his eyes, the dumbass turned and peed on my boots."

Before he could continue, Sophie burst into laughter. Her entire face changed when she laughed. Her eyes filled with light as she tossed her head back, the smooth column of her neck now visible, her perky breasts pushed forward in that tight button-down shirt. He shifted in his chair, trying to subtly rearrange his erection. When she finally calmed herself, he found that he was grinning too. She wiped tears from her eyes and smiled at him, like they now shared some private joke.

"So I had to go into the bar to clean the piss off of my

shoes, but I was stopped on my way to the bathroom by this hot-ass blonde in a skimpy, white dress. Seriously, you should have seen this babe. Legs for days—" Sophie interrupted before he could wax poetic about the woman's ass, which, to be honest, he hadn't even paid an ounce of attention to.

She cleared her throat, those gorgeous green eyes shooting daggers at him across the table. *If looks could kill*, Rafe thought with a self-satisfied smirk. "Mr. Pierce, I don't see how this is in any way relevant to the story. Could you move on please?"

"Oh, right. Sorry about that, doll." He grinned, shooting her another wink. Her eyes narrowed and her lips tightened. He could've sworn he saw her fingers twitch as she clearly fought the urge to slap him and storm off. "Anyway, so this chick thought I was the stripper for her bachelorette party. I mean, can you blame the girl?" He gestured at his body and gave her a lascivious grin. She rolled her eyes again, but managed to hold back whatever snarky comment she wanted to make. He honestly didn't know how she did it. The poor girl looked like she was literally biting her tongue. "I very politely corrected her." Sophie couldn't hold in the scoff this time. "And she asked for my picture. Must've wanted something for her spank bank." He shrugged.

"Delightful. So that's the whole story?" Sophie asked, clearly wanting to wrap this up and get the hell away from him. He found himself wanting the interview to continue, surprisingly. He was having a blast saying any outrageous thing he could think of just to annoy her. He couldn't help it if she looked sexy as hell when she was pissed off.

"Well, yeah, pretty much. I mean, I considered taking one of the bride's friends with me to the bathroom..." He winked again. "But I was on duty so I just washed off my boots and went back outside."

Apparently Sophie had had enough. She stopped the recording app on her phone and stood. "Well, as *fun* as this has been," she paused to glare, "I think I have everything I need. Thank you for your cooperation, Mr. Pierce."

He made a show of looking disappointed before pointedly checking out her rack. The reporter had nice tits, he couldn't deny that. He raised his eyes to hers and quirked a brow before saying something he knew would keep her from asking for another interview.

"You want to take this back to my place? I can think of some things we could *record*."

Oh, he'd done it now. Sophie's nostrils flared and her eyes widened in shock before narrowing on him once more. She prowled over to him, and the glare she gave him had his boys shriveling up in his jeans. He'd expected her to slap him, honestly. What he didn't expect was for the scowl to fall from her face while her lips quirked into a flirtatious smile. She patted him on the cheek, that sugar-sweet smile still gracing her pink lips, and leaned over to whisper something in his ear that had him hard and ready to go in record time.

"Oh, bless your heart," she whispered. "You couldn't handle a night with me. You'd be better off sticking to badge bunnies." She patted his cheek and closed his mouth for him before walking away.

CHAPTER FOUR

"SO HOW HOT was this cop, really? Because in the picture I've seen the dude looks entirely too fuckable," Sophie's friend Becky asked that night over wine and cult classics. It was a tradition that had started when she, Becky, and Kelsey were roommates in college. Without fail, the three of them got together once a week to gossip and drink wine while cult classic movies played in the background. In honor of tonight's movie, *Mean Girls*, the three of them were, of course, wearing pink.

Kelsey did an actual spit take, her wine coating Sophie's coffee table as she burst out laughing at Becky's question. Sophie grabbed a roll of paper towels from the side table next to her and passed them to Kelsey. Unfortunately for her furniture, spit takes were a pretty regular occurrence on cult classic night. Becky tended to say whatever popped into her head. The woman really had no filter. It was one of the things Sophie loved the most about her.

When Kelsey had finished cleaning up the mess, she

turned to Sophie with an impatient stare. "Well? Answer the question! Inquiring minds need to know, Soph."

She sighed and brought up the image of Rafe in her mind. Dark blonde hair, piercing blue eyes, and a panty-dropping smile? Fuckable was an understatement. The things she wanted to do to him would make a porn star blush. "Yes, he was that hot in person. That's the problem though. The guy was a complete and total prick! You should've heard the things he said to me. I mean, who the hell talks about other women's asses in an *interview*?"

Kelsey's eyes widened. "You're lying. There is no way he did that."

Sophie knew that she wasn't supposed to share recordings of her interviews, but these were her best friends, and they needed to hear this. She reached forward and grabbed her phone, unlocking it and pulling up the recording app. She scrolled through the interview with her thumb and scrolled forward until she'd reached the last ten minutes. She hit play and turned the speaker toward her friends. She actually shivered as Rafe's sexy, deep voice came through the speaker. It wasn't fair, really. How could a man look that good and have a voice that sexy?

When the recording ended, Kelsey looked appalled and Becky was practically drooling. "That voice!" she said excitedly. "Can you imagine phone sex with a guy like that? I'm sliding off my seat just thinking about it." Becky made a point of fanning her face while actually sliding off of the leather love seat she was perched on.

Sophie laughed and threw a pillow at her friend. "Don't encourage me, Becky. This is the kind of guy I'm supposed to stay away from, remember?"

"I mean, a little fun wouldn't hurt you. You haven't had

sex since you kicked Charlie out two years ago. How many vibrators are you going to break before you finally decide to get some actual dick?"

Sophie sighed and looked to Kelsey for support. She was the more reserved of her two friends and could always be counted on to be the voice of reason. Unfortunately, it looked like Sophie was on her own this time. Kelsey was looking down at her phone, a slight blush staining her cheeks. She had a feeling she knew what her friend was looking at.

Her suspicion was confirmed when Kelsey turned her phone around. There, in full color, was a picture of Rafe. He had a sexy, genuine smile on his face, and his arm was wrapped around a handsome Latino man. He looked a few years younger, but just as handsome in his police uniform.

"Oh come on, Kelsey, not you too." Sophie groaned, tearing her eyes away from the photo. "Where did you even find that picture?"

Her friend threw her a sheepish smile. "It's from his police academy graduation; one of the news stations shared it online. Sorry, Soph, but I'm with Becky. I mean after two years, doesn't your hymen grow back? Are there cobwebs down there?"

Sophie buried her face in the armrest of her chair and groaned. "My hymen hasn't grown back, you assholes. I need a nice guy to break my dry spell. Trust me, Rafe is far from *nice*."

Her friends fell silent for a moment and the three of them turned to watch Tina Fey pull off her shirt in front of her entire classroom. Sophie took a big sip of wine and said the one thing she knew would make her friends forget all about Rafe.

"What if I let you two make a Tinder profile for me instead?"

Becky and Kelsey's grins were downright maniacal. Sophie handed her phone over to Kelsey while Becky went to the kitchen to grab another bottle of wine. Tonight was going to be a long night.

Sophie woke up the next morning with a massive hangover. She moaned and rolled over, feeling around her nightstand for her phone. When she finally found it, she pulled it under the covers with her and hit the home button so she could see what time it was.

Eight in the morning—seriously? Stupid internal alarm clock, it's Sunday.

Figuring she might as well get up and get her errands out of the way, she took a quick shower and pulled on dark-wash skinny jeans and a comfy off-the-shoulder sweater. Not even bothering with makeup or a hair dryer, she had her purse on her shoulder and was out the door twenty minutes later. She would just get her errands out of the way before spending the afternoon with pajamas and a *Friends* marathon. She had a trunk full of clothes to donate to Goodwill, and she still wanted to pick out a birthday present for Becky. One of their cult classic Saturdays would be spent clubbing in a couple months, and Sophie wanted to get her best friend's present early. Fortunately, the Goodwill in Montrose was neighbor to a row of quirky clothing boutiques. A fun dress and a smutty book was always a safe bet with Becky.

First order of business though was coffee. The pounding in her head had yet to subside. Wine was her drink of choice, but after the three bottles she and her friends had downed last night, she had a pounding headache that could only be cured by a bone-dry cappuccino. She pulled into the parking lot of her favorite Montrose coffee shop, just a few blocks away from the stores she planned to visit.

Unfortunately, she didn't appear to be the only person in dire need of coffee this morning. Sophie sighed and got into line, pulling up the Sunday edition of the *Houston Reporter* on her phone. Her feature on Texas Children's Hospital had been published today, and seeing her byline never failed to bring a smile to her face. She had just finished reading her piece when a throat cleared loudly behind her. She turned around and was met with the sweat-dampened chest of one Rafe Pierce.

He was clearly coming from a run or workout, and his white T-shirt was soaked through, showcasing spectacular pecs and a washboard stomach. Instead of tearing her gaze away from his chest, like she should've done, Sophie's eyes traced the dips and curves of his muscles, working their way down to his abs.

Of course he has a six-pack. Perfect.

Before her eyes could explore any lower, Rafe cleared his throat again and crossed his arms over his chest, drawing her attention to his defined biceps before she worked her gaze up to his face.

His eyes sparkled and his lips were tipped up in a self-satisfied smile. "Like what you see, doll?"

Ugh, does he have to be such a smug asshole?

Letting her eyes wander once more, she intentionally focused below his waistband for a few moments before meeting his cool blue gaze once more.

She shrugged and smiled. "Meh, I've seen better actually. You're not all that…impressive."

To her surprise, he threw back his head and laughed. "Oh, sweetheart. You haven't seen anything yet."

"Yet? Trust me, *Mr. Pierce*," she said, once again emphasizing his last name. "You don't have anything I want to see."

He leaned forward, his lips right next to her ear. She could feel his hot breath on her neck, and her breasts suddenly felt heavy, her nipples hardening to points under her shirt. "Considering the eye-fucking you just gave me, I think I have plenty you want to see," he said, voice going deep and husky with desire.

She tried to come up with a response, but her mouth couldn't seem to form words. A witty comeback stuck in her throat, and, instead, a low moan escaped her mouth when he leaned forward just a bit more, his nose nuzzling the tender spot under her ear. She glanced down once more and saw something quite impressive indeed stirring in his shorts.

Before she could do something stupid, like actually kiss the asshole, the barista behind the counter called for the next person in line. Sophie stepped back quickly, putting space between herself and Rafe. He shook his head and stood up straight once more, reaching down to obviously situate himself, *in public*, while quirking an eyebrow at her.

She huffed and turned to place her order, feeling Rafe move to stand behind her. When she laid eyes on Rafe, the barista perked right up.

"Rafe! Hi!" she said excitedly. The poor girl couldn't have been older than twenty-one and was practically vibrating with excitement. She completely ignored Sophie and turned to pour a cup of dark roast into a to-go mug for Rafe instead.

"Hey, Tiffany," he replied, glancing at Sophie before winking at the barista. The poor girl tittered, actually *tittered*, and handed him his coffee.

"It's on the house," she breathed, cheeks pink and eyes practically glazed.

Sick of waiting, Sophie sighed and crossed her arms over her chest. "Can you just get it over with and give him your number so I can get my damn coffee?"

Tiffany looked startled to realize Sophie was actually there, and blushed. "I'm so sorry, ma'am. What can I get for you?"

She gave the barista her coffee order and credit card before turning to Rafe. "Are you quite done now? You have your coffee, feel free to leave at anytime."

"Do I sense jealousy, doll?"

"Oh absolutely," she drawled. "I've always wanted to be a notch on someone's bed post."

"Then I'll be sure to save some room for you on mine." He winked one final time before sauntering out of the coffee shop, leaving Sophie pissed off and way too aroused for her own good. Maybe she would pick up a new vibrator before she went home.

CHAPTER FIVE

SOPHIE SPENT all of Monday morning working on her "Hot Cop" piece. After the run-in at the coffee shop yesterday, she'd run her errands as quickly as possible before heading home with her new toy. As if it wasn't bad enough that Rafe had popped into her fantasies last night, she now had to spend the whole day listening to his deep, sexy baritone while working on her feature.

When she'd completed her work and edited it, she sent it to Karen and began to sort through the stories she had yet to copyedit. While she did write her own pieces, she enjoyed editing more and had stayed on as one of the newspaper's senior copyeditors. She was working on her second story when she received a text from Karen telling her to come to her office.

The moment she walked into her boss's office, she knew she was in for it. Karen motioned for her to sit down, and steepled her hands under her chin, fixing Sophie with a stare that had made grown men spill their guts. Sophie did her best not to fidget, determined not to be the first person to talk.

Finally, Karen sighed and leaned back. "What the hell is this?" she asked, throwing a printed copy of Sophie's article on the desk between them. "I asked you for a feature, not a scathing article about how much of a womanizer the guy is."

"You should've seen the guy, Karen! He gave me nothing. He actually said that he joined the force for the ladies. How am I supposed to spin that into anything else?"

Karen fixed her with a hard stare. "You and I both know that you can do better. I don't want a scathing article about how much of a prick Raphael Pierce is. This guy is Houston's hot hero. I want to know more. I want to know the *real* reason he became a cop."

"I just couldn't get it out of him," Sophie said, frustrated. She knew where this conversation was going and she was not looking forward to it.

"I made a call to Officer Pierce's captain today. I want a real story, Sophie. You're going to be shadowing him for the next two weeks. I want a *series* of pieces about this guy. His captain says he's one of the best they have; I want to know why. The women of this city are dying to know more about Raphael Pierce, and you're going to give it to them."

Sophie groaned and opened her mouth to argue but was cut off. "I'm serious, Sophie. Finish all of your copyedits today and tomorrow. Wednesday you're expected to be at the HPD station in Montrose at 5 p.m. sharp. Pierce and his partner are on the night shift."

Sophie mumbled her agreement and headed back to her desk to get to work. Today was going to be a long day. She had a mountain of stories to edit and one day to complete them. She needed more coffee.

As she was leaving work late that night, she heard her phone ringing in her purse, the song "This is Me" from *The Greatest Showman* blaring in the quiet of the parking garage. She was going to kill Kelsey for setting that as her ringtone. Kels had called her during a copyeditor meeting last week, and she was still getting hell for her ringtone choice. Digging through her purse, she snagged the phone and swiped to answer, tucking it against her ear while resuming her walk to the car.

"Hey Kels!"

"Sophie," Kelsey said, her voice thick with tears. "James and I need to come stay with you for a little while. Is that okay?"

"Of course, it is! What's going on, though? Are you okay?"

Kelsey started sobbing, the choked noise coming through the phone. "I left Kyle and he didn't take it well. I just need to get out of here, please."

"Oh, Kelsey, you have a spare key. Go let yourself in, get James settled in the guest room, and I'll pick up some wine on my way home. I love you and I'll see you soon, okay?"

Kelsey's muffled "okay" made it through the phone before she hung up.

Twenty minutes later, Sophie walked through the front door to her house. Dropping her purse and the bottles of wine on the table in the entry, she walked over to the couch and wrapped her best friend in a huge hug. Kelsey had stopped crying, but there was a box of tissues on the coffee table, and her eyes were red and puffy.

"Kels, I knew you and Kyle were in marriage counseling, but what happened?"

Kelsey released Sophie and leaned back on the couch cushions. "I think I was promised wine?"

Sophie laughed and got up, quickly retrieving a bottle of wine from the entry and grabbing two glasses from her kitchen. After Kelsey had taken a fortifying sip of their favorite vintage of red, she sucked in a deep breath and started speaking.

"Kyle and I were college sweethearts, you know? When I met him, I thought he was just so incredible, and for those first few years, everything was perfect. I mean the sex was off-the-charts hot, and he was so much fun to be around."

Sophie nodded. She'd been there when Kelsey had met Kyle at a frat party freshman year. They had been such a golden couple.

"Then when I got pregnant with James during our senior year, everything changed. We got married so quickly, and everything I wanted for myself kind of fell away. Suddenly I was twenty-two years old and married with a kid. Kyle focused on work, and I stayed home to raise James, and we just grew into completely different people. I've tried to feel something, to fall back in love with him, but those people? Those two young kids who were so in love? They just don't exist anymore. I will always love Kyle, but I couldn't keep trying to convince myself that I was in love with him."

"Kelsey, I had no idea. Why didn't you tell me you were feeling this way?"

"I've been convincing myself for so long that it was my fault. That I was just romanticizing our early years, wanting some Hollywood romance that didn't exist. But I miss working and having a career and a life of my own. I wouldn't trade James for anything, I love him so much. I just need more out of my life."

Sophie nodded, refilling Kelsey's wineglass and urging her to continue.

"Anyway, I tried to tell Kyle that a few weeks ago. I asked to go back to work, even part-time. I found this great graphic design position that I knew I would be perfect for, but he shut me down. He said he wouldn't even consider it and that I was being selfish. I've been working up the courage to ask for a divorce since that night. I got my ducks in a row, consulted a lawyer, and had papers drawn up. He was served them tonight, and he was so angry. I just had to get out of there, and you were the first person I thought to call."

"Well you came to the right place. Stay here as long as you need to."

"Thank you so much, Sophie. I don't know what I would do without you." Kelsey hugged Sophie again before downing her glass of wine. "Now please tell me you got more than one bottle? This is more of a four bottle kind of conversation."

"Oh ye of little faith, I bought five bottles. How dare you underestimate me."

CHAPTER SIX

RAMIREZ MOANED as he bit into his Reuben sandwich. Loudly. The girls at the next table looked over and giggled, eyeing Rafe and Carlos with interest. Carlos looked up from his meal at the sound and, with a mouth full of sandwich, winked at them.

Rafe threw a fry across the table, nailing his partner in the forehead. "Dude, are you fucking serious?"

"What?" Carlos asked innocently, taking another large bite of his meal and reaching over to steal a fry from Rafe.

"Do you really have to make love to your food in public? Keep moaning like that and people are going to think I'm giving you a foot job under the table."

Carlos lifted his eyebrows suggestively. "Why, Officer Pierce…" he said in a high voice. "Are you hitting on me?"

Rafe rolled his eyes and smacked Carlos's hand away from his plate as he tried to steal a fry. It had been a pretty quiet patrol night so far. Tuesdays weren't particularly busy in Houston. He and Carlos had stopped at his favorite Jewish deli for a quick bite before heading back out.

He raised his head to flag their waiter down when the front door opened and he spotted her. Sophie Klein was looking *damn* good tonight. Her blonde hair was piled on top of her head in a messy bun held together with a pencil. She had on a mint green cardigan over a silk polka-dot shirt. The shirt wasn't tight but was just sheer enough for Rafe to glimpse the cup of her white bra. Black dress pants encased her long legs, hugging her ass perfectly. But the best part? She was wearing black fuck-me heels.

Jesus, does the woman own any flats?

Those heels gave him ideas. Made him want to take her home, pin her to the wall, and fuck her in nothing but those damn shoes. He felt his dick hardening in his polyester work pants. Not an ideal situation. His duty belt would make it impossible to hide. Tucking his dick into his waistband was not an option in this uniform.

Before he could think twice about it, Rafe was out of his seat and making his way over to Sophie. He tore his eyes away from her ass as he approached the to-go stand and thought long and hard about baseball stats, willing his erection to disappear. By the time he was standing behind her, he was still rocking a semi, but it was manageable.

He leaned over her shoulder to peer at the menu she was holding, and whispered in her ear, "I hear they have great sausage here."

Sophie started and turned around. Her big green eyes widened for a brief moment before narrowing on him in a glare he was starting to think she reserved just for him.

"Stalk much?" she huffed, crossing her arms over her chest, drawing his gaze down.

Bad move, sweetheart. Your tits look great when you do that.

He returned his eyes to her face. She looked stressed today.

There was tension in her shoulders, and her mascara was a bit smeared, like she'd been rubbing her eyes all day. He couldn't explain it, but he had the sudden urge to make her smile.

"Hey, you're in my part of town, remember? First you come into *my* coffee shop, and now you're interrupting my dinner break. Do I need to file a restraining order? Or are you just trying to goad me into using my cuffs on you?"

Her nostrils flared and she took a step forward, poking him in the chest. "In. Your. Dreams," she said, a poke emphasizing each word.

"Oh, there is no doubt about it. I *absolutely* dream about you in handcuffs. Just last night, I dreamed you were handcuffed to that bedpost you seem to think has so many notches. You were naked and I was licking your—"

She cut him off before he could finish, "You are such a perv." Her words lacked any heat, her cheeks flushing and eyes clouding with desire. Her breasts were rising and falling with each breath and he couldn't help himself. He stared. Hard. Shit, polyester had no give and his erection was back in full force. He winced as the zipper of his pants pressed against his throbbing dick.

What is happening to me? I'm popping boners like a damn teenager. In fucking public. Could this get any worse?

He looked up when she started laughing. Her eyes lit with humor as she looked down at his pants. "That looks mighty uncomfortable for you, Mr. Pierce."

He growled. "You have no idea." He needed to stop staring at her tits. He just couldn't help himself, and her shirt was making things worse. How could a woman look so good in dress pants and a damn cardigan? The view he was getting of her lacy bra was giving him ideas, and a series of images flashed through his mind. He groaned and lifted his eyes to the ceiling.

She laughed again and, not wanting to miss it, Rafe returned his gaze to her face.

Son of a bitch.

While he'd been thinking about baseball stats again, she'd pulled the pen from her hair and was now running her fingers through it. It fell in loose waves around her shoulders, making him wonder what it would look like spread across his pillow. Rafe was just about to ask her to button her cardigan, or at least put her damn hair back up, when he felt a hand on his shoulder.

"Hey asshole, I paid the bill for dinner. Thanks for leaving me with that, by the way. Are you at least going to introduce me to your friend?"

The only good thing about Carlos joining them was that the moment the man's hand had landed on his shoulder, his dick deflated. He was going to have a serious case of blue balls later.

Before he could tell Carlos to fuck off, Sophie stuck her hand out. "I'm Sophie Klein, the reporter who'll be doing a piece on Officer Pierce."

"Ohhh, Officer Pretty Boy gets his own story in a newspaper? Why didn't you mention this sooner, Rafe?"

Sophie looked between the two of them in confusion. "Wait, you don't know about the series of articles I'll be writing? I'll be tailing both of you for the next two weeks working on this."

That got Rafe's attention quickly. "No, no, no, doll. You've already gotten your interview. You must be mistaken. Besides, how the hell do you plan to ride around in a cop car with the *two* of us when there is no back seat? That partition isn't just for show, you know."

Sophie's brow furrowed. "My boss talked to your captain today. I'm supposed to report to the station at five tomorrow evening for your shift."

Hell no. The last thing he needed was a reporter digging into his past. He didn't need that shit broadcasted, and he sure as hell didn't want to be the subject of *multiple* articles. He and the captain were about to have a serious discussion.

Rafe's discussion with the captain did not go well. He was more or less told that he would take Sophie on two weeks' worth of ride-alongs and be happy about it, or he could shove his police cruiser somewhere anatomically impossible. He stomped into the locker room, shucking off his civilian clothes and throwing them roughly into his locker. As he tugged on his uniform, his partner, Ramirez, sauntered in, all smiles and swagger. Did the guy ever stop smiling? He was a walking advertisement for fucking Prozac.

"So I hear that sexy-ass reporter *will* be riding around with us for the next couple weeks." Carlos grinned, opening his own locker and pulling on his uniform.

Rafe grunted, not in the mood to deal with his overenthusiastic, flirt-with-anything-that-moves partner.

"I don't know what you're so upset about. We finally get to ride in one of the big boy cars! No more police cruiser for us. Bring on the Ford Explorer, baby."

"Do you even know how much of a pain in the ass this is going to be? We won't get any interesting calls for two fucking weeks. It's going to be all traffic stops and fucking parking tickets. And if we do need to arrest someone? We have to call out a damn patrol unit because we won't have a cage in the back."

"Pretty boy, I think you're forgetting the upside to all of this. We get to ride in a new SUV, one that doesn't smell like piss, with a girl I *know* you want to sleep with. You should be absolutely giddy."

"I don't want to sleep with her," Rafe grumbled, feeling downright petulant.

Carlos guffawed, slapping Rafe on the back and leaving him in the locker room.

CHAPTER SEVEN

SOPHIE WAS both dreading and anticipating tonight. Starting work at 5 p.m. definitely had its perks. Kelsey and James staying with her was amazing, but Sophie was used to having the house to herself, not waking up at 5 a.m. to a screaming two-year-old. Her godson was damn lucky he was cute, because the kid could wail. As it turned out, there was not enough coffee in the world to make waking up at 5 a.m. acceptable. So, while Kelsey had taken James to the children's museum, Sophie had taken a deliciously long afternoon nap.

She was fully refreshed and still not at all prepared to deal with Rafe for the next eight hours. She had already used her vibrator six times since purchasing it, and without fail, every time she was about to orgasm, that smug, grinning face popped into her head. Sophie shook the memory of those orgasms off and got out of her car, straightening her sleeveless button-down over her dark-wash jeans. She had dressed down for the ride-along, but was unwilling to give up her heels. She already had to look up to Rafe; she was not going to make it worse by wearing flats.

The moment she walked into the station, a boisterous voice excitedly yelled her name. She looked up to see Carlos's broad-shouldered form making its way over to her. He slung his arm around her shoulder like they were already best friends.

"Hiya, shortcake! Get it? Because you're so short? You're like my very own Strawberry Shortcake!"

"Thanks, I hadn't noticed. But now that you've pointed it out, I do feel shorter than average," she replied drolly.

Before Carlos could come up with some smart-assed reply, Rafe strolled over, that charming swagger present in his walk. His gaze slowly worked its way down her body, one eyebrow arching when it landed on the stilettos she was wearing. He looked back up at her and winked, the bastard.

"So you wore heels for me, huh?" He grinned, leaning lazily against the reception counter.

Carlos's arm dropped from around Sophie's shoulder as he looked between the two of them.

"Whoaaaa, hold up, motherfucker. You're not supposed to be the charming one. You're the Eeyore to my Tigger. Knock it the hell off."

Rafe scowled and stood up straight, a dour expression falling over his features. "I'm perfectly charming, you asshole. Can we go now?" Rafe asked, walking away from the pair of them.

Carlos leaned down and stage-whispered, "He's a little grumpy today, didn't get to have his Wheaties this morning." Sophie laughed and followed Carlos outside to join Rafe. At least she would like one person on this ride-along.

They were walking out to the SUV, Carlos chattering

excitedly about the "big boy car" they'd be riding in, when he stopped suddenly, tugging on her arm and pulling her toward an older gentleman getting into his own car.

"Cap! Hey Cap, did you meet our resident reporter? She's gonna tell all of Houston how irresistibly charming I am, aren't ya, shortcake?"

Sophie stuck her hand out. "Sophie Klein from the *Houston Reporter*. Nice to meet you."

"Ah, you're the one doing a story on our illustrious Officer Pierce. Best of luck with that one. I have a feeling he'll be tough to crack. Ramirez, don't fuck around on this ride-along. Wouldn't want you getting killed because you couldn't stop staring at the pretty lady long enough to do your job."

Carlos scoffed. "You should be more worried about her staring at me. I mean, come on, the girl is practically eye-fucking me as we speak, Cap. I'll be pregnant in no time if she keeps this up."

The captain ignored Carlos's rambling, turning to get into his car. "Nice to meet you, Ms. Klein. Oh, and Ramirez, before I forget, change of schedule this week. You and Pierce take tomorrow off. You'll be working twelves Friday, Saturday, and Sunday to cover the music festival."

"Awww, Cap, I had a date this weekend," Carlos groaned. The captain got in his car and closed the door, pretending not to hear the complaint.

They had been on patrol for seven hours now and nothing had happened. Absolutely fucking nothing. Sophie had to wonder how many hours of footage they had to tape to get even one hour of action for the show *Cops*. So far, they had pulled over three people—one for speeding and two for running red lights. Aside from the boredom, the only constants in the car were Carlos's rambling and Rafe's shitty attitude. He had yet to answer a single one of her questions with more than one syllable. The majority of his responses came in the form of noncommittal grunts. The conversation would go something like this:

"Officer Pierce, did you grow up in the Houston area?"

Grunt that semi-resembled a yes in response.

"Have you always known you wanted to be on the force?"

Shrug of shoulders and noncommittal grunt.

"Officer Pierce, should I jump out of the moving vehicle and leave you the fuck alone?"

Brief head nod, shrug of shoulders, grunt.

At one point in the "interview" Carlos had taken pity on Sophie and just started answering questions as if they were being asked of him. Sophie didn't know jack shit about Rafe, but she knew Carlos's entire life story, down to his first kiss in what he claimed was high school. Sophie theorized that it was more likely in college.

With thirty minutes remaining in the ride-along, Rafe pulled the patrol vehicle into the precinct parking lot. He had removed the keys from the ignition and was getting out of the SUV before Sophie found her voice.

"Wait, we still have a half hour. Why are we getting out?"

Rafe glanced over his shoulder and graced her with the most words she'd heard from him in the last seven hours: "Slow night, you can leave now."

Sophie wasn't sure if it was the grunts and shrugs he'd thrown her way all night or the disregard with which he treated her interview, but she lost it.

"Are you fucking kidding me? You have been *less* than helpful all night. I have nothing for my interview and now we're ending the shift early? I don't know about you, but I have a goddamn job to do."

Carlos looked rapidly between the two of them, his eyes widening as he slowly unbuckled his seatbelt and opened the door to the SUV. He shut the door and backed away with his hands in the air, keeping up the charade until he reached the door of the station.

Sophie followed his lead and got out of the car, circling the vehicle so that she could stand toe to toe with Rafe.

"You know, I think I preferred it when you were a womanizing asshole. At least then you answered my fucking questions," she said, poking him in the chest.

"Sorry I didn't meet your expectations tonight, sweetheart. Maybe you should find some other fluff piece to write. This is me—I come to work, get shit done, and go home. I don't know what salacious gossip you were looking for, but I've got nothing for you."

"Salacious gossip? I'm an actual reporter. I write real news."

Rafe laughed. "Oh yeah I saw that piece you did earlier this year about the Easter Egg hunt in Eleanor Tinsley Park. Real hard-hitting stuff; you must've worked so hard to write that one. I imagine your investigative skills were really put to use trying to figure out how many eggs they hid."

Sophie raised her arm to slap him, her hand almost reaching his face, when he caught her wrist. That stupid fucking smirk was firmly back in place when he spat, "Are you sure you want to assault a police officer on government property?"

Sophie would've loved to say she'd come up with some witty retort, but what came out of her mouth was simply, "Fuck you, Rafe." Without even throwing a second glance over her shoulder, she stormed to her car. He was still standing by the SUV when she pulled out of the parking lot, Sophie fighting the very strong urge to run him the hell over.

CHAPTER EIGHT

A SCREAMING CHILD woke Sophie the next morning at promptly 5:17 a.m. In her sleep-deprived state, she swatted at her alarm clock in the hopes it would silence the awful noise. When the baby continued to cry, Sophie pulled the pillow out from under her and shoved it over her face, trying this time to muffle the wails.

Twenty minutes later, Sophie surrendered, allowing James to win this round. She stumbled into the kitchen where Kelsey was feeding James Cheerios with one hand (Cheerios, which he proceeded to throw across her kitchen) and mainlining coffee with the other. Not even bothering to get her own mug, Sophie swiped the coffee straight from Kelsey's hand and drained the cup in one gulp.

"Chum! What the hell?" Kelsey said, referencing an all-time favorite book series of theirs. "Get me a new cup of coffee before I feed you to a goddamn lanima."

"Your *Illuminae* references have no bearing on this conversation. It is five a.m. and I hate you so, so, so much right now. I didn't get home from the ride-along from hell until after two. And now, your demon-spawn has woken me up before the sun is even up."

"Calm your tits, it's almost six. Wait, why was the ride-along so awful?"

"Well first of all, Rafe has this annoying-ass partner. Every time I asked Rafe a question, Carlos had to jump in and answer it himself. Not exactly helpful. But I don't even know if I can fault the guy; Rafe's answers were all monosyllabic. I can't even imagine how painful it would've been to witness."

Kelsey laughed. "Sounds like this Carlos guy is just trying to help you out."

"This coffee isn't strong enough, Kels. Do you think it's too early for wine?"

"Hmmm, if you hadn't gone to sleep yet, you could just call it a bender and drink all day. But you just woke up, so maybe you should wait a few more hours. If you can make it for twelve hours, we can go to happy hour with Becky. Kyle asked to take James tonight, something about a family dinner."

"Sounds like a plan. Now do me a favor and shut my adorable godson up so I can get some fucking sleep."

Twelve hours, three sushi platters, and four sake bombs later, Sophie was in a *much* better mood. After dinner, they had decided to go to their favorite dive bar in the Montrose area for craft beer. This particular bar had over fifty beers on draft and a gorgeous patio complete with hammocks. On weekends, they would use a projector to play old movies on the side of the building, but on a regular Thursday night, it was packed. After their second round of drinks, Kelsey and Sophie were sharing a hammock and not so silently judging the drunks, while Becky had wandered off to join some random hottie in a hammock of their own.

Sophie had almost forgotten about her disastrous interview, when one drunk idiot in particular caught her attention. Carlos had a giant dopey grin on his face as he walked toward her and Kelsey.

"Shortcake," he exclaimed cheerfully. "Hurry up and introduce me to your friend with the killer legs."

Sophie sighed and rolled her eyes, but before she could get to the introduction, Kelsey got out of the hammock and stuck her hand out. "Based entirely on that conversation alone, I'm guessing you must be Carlos."

Shock flitted across Carlos's face before it broke into a gleeful smile. "Talking me up already, huh? Watch out, Rafe will get jealous if he hears you singing my praises."

At Rafe's name, Sophie immediately felt herself stiffen.

Please don't let him be here, please don't let him be here.

"He's over at the bar if you want to try slapping him again. He isn't in uniform this time so it wouldn't be *as* big of a crime."

The sentence was barely out of his mouth before Sophie started moving. Storming toward the bar, she belatedly felt a little bad for leaving Kelsey alone to deal with Carlos.

Rafe was, of course, easy to spot. The man looked like an out-of-place Hemsworth brother with a stick up his ass. Seriously, who sat up that straight at a bar? Apparently not even hard liquor was capable of loosening his posture.

In a moment she would later look back on as not her finest, Sophie tapped him on the shoulder. She barely let the shock of seeing her register on his face before she slapped him, hard enough to stop all conversation at the bar top.

A shocked guffaw burst out of his mouth, quickly turning

into outright laughter. Sophie realized that she had yet to see him genuinely laugh. His eyes crinkled and his head was thrown back as his shoulders heaved. When he finally managed to contain himself long enough to take her in, she saw something wholly unexpected in his eyes. Heat. Rafe was looking at her like he wanted to absolutely devour her, and though she knew she should be pissed at him, she felt her body responding. Her breasts suddenly felt heavy in the strapless summer dress she was wearing, and her nipples hardened to points.

Rafe's eyes dipped to her chest and he licked his lips as he took in the sight. Maybe tonight hadn't been the best night to go braless. Without saying a word, Rafe finished his drink, placed the empty glass on the bar top, and grabbed her hand. A mix of desire and shock had her following him across the bar in the direction of the restrooms. She was about to protest, when he pulled open a door she hadn't noticed and pushed her into what appeared to be a storage closet. The door hadn't even completely closed before his mouth was on hers.

He kissed her like a starving man, like he needed the air in her lungs to breathe. One hand pushed through her hair, grasping the back of her neck, while the other slid down her body. Everywhere he touched sparked at the contact. His hand moved slowly down her side, caressing the side of her breast, her waist, and then her hip before sliding around to grab her ass. He cupped her firmly in one palm and tugged her forward, pressing his chest against hers.

All the while, he continued kissing her, first in teasing nips and then deeper, sliding his tongue into her mouth, exploring it before twining it with her own. He slowly walked her backwards until her back met the wall of the small closet. Sophie's body was on fire, her nerves tingling, her panties soaked. He released his hold on the back of her neck, and used both hands to wrap her legs around his waist, supporting her with one hand under her ass. He began grinding into her, his hard cock hitting just the right spot, making Sophie moan.

Rafe released her mouth and trailed kisses down her throat, using his free hand to pull down the top of her dress. She tunneled her hands into his hair as his mouth dipped lower, taking one nipple into his mouth. Sophie cried out as he lightly bit down, soothing the sting with a swipe of his tongue. He moved to the other breast and was laving her nipple with broad strokes of his tongue when she felt his hand slip under her dress and into her thong.

He pushed the fabric aside, running one finger up her slit to find her clit. "Fuck, Sophie. You're so wet," he growled. He slid one finger into her, while his thumb teased the bundle of nerves. She was gasping for breath now, moaning loudly enough that she was sure anyone walking by the closet could hear her.

"I can't wait anymore," Rafe murmured. His hand left her and she heard his zipper, followed by the crinkling of a condom wrapper.

"Rafe, yes..." she moaned, too lost in the moment to care about the fact that she hated him. She needed him inside her *now*.

Before she had even finished the thought, he thrust into her, burying his face in her neck. He stayed still for a moment, giving her time to get used to his sudden intrusion before he started moving. God, did he move. Rafe pinned her to the wall with both hands on her hips and fucked her like a man unhinged. There was no doubt in Sophie's mind, no disillusionment—this was raw, animal lust. As he pounded into her, his thumb returned to her clit, stroking it in small circles.

He silenced her moans with a hard kiss, to which she responded with a bite. There was no finesse in their kissing now. They were ravenous for each other, the ferocity of their kissing matching the fast pace Rafe set as he drove into her.

"Fuck, you feel so good. Come for me, Sophie. Fucking come for me," Rafe rasped, his breath catching. Sophie could tell he was close; she was too. He nipped her earlobe and whispered one more time, "Come for me, now."

That was all it took. Sophie's orgasm hit her like a lightning strike, racing through her body. She felt Rafe shudder as she came, and he moaned her name as he followed her.

Afterwards, they stayed that way for a moment longer, both of them panting, Rafe still inside her, before she wiggled to get down. Sophie pulled her dress up to cover her breasts and did her best to smooth her hair. The last thing she needed was for Carlos and Kelsey to notice her disheveled state and ask questions.

Rafe pulled off the condom and wrapped it in a paper towel (the one good thing about supply-closet sex—the supplies) before tucking it in his pocket. Once he had zipped back up, Sophie opened the door to leave. She looked over her shoulder, the light from the hallway shining on Rafe's face. His hair was standing on end from her fingers, and his lips were kiss swollen. He looked devastatingly handsome, but he still hadn't apologized to her for the way he'd insulted her career. He started to open his mouth to say something, when she cut him off.

"Never again," she said fiercely. Sophie turned around

and left him there, standing in the supply closet, with their used condom still in his pocket. She needed to find Kelsey and get the hell out of here.

Sophie woke up Friday morning to the blissful sound of silence. She stretched out, unfolding her limbs and basking in the warm sunlight filtering through the windows. Kelsey's ex-husband would have James until Monday, leaving Kelsey with three full days of sleeping in. Because Sophie wouldn't be shadowing Rafe and Carlos on music festival duty, her boss had assigned her a feature on the bands playing this weekend. June in Houston would definitely be miserable, but some of her favorite bands were performing, and she was really looking forward to her weekend. Her blessedly Rafe-free weekend.

What the hell had happened last night? One minute she was pissed at him, the next he was inside her. The sex had been incredible, easily the best she'd ever had. She had never had such a powerful orgasm with so little foreplay. Something about the raw power in Rafe as he had fucked her set her off, and she felt herself flush just thinking about it. She was about to reach into her bedside table and pull out her vibrator when she heard a laugh. A distinctly masculine and somewhat familiar laugh. She had to be mistaken; there was no way Kelsey had brought home *Carlos* of all people.

Last night when Sophie had left the storage closet, she'd gone in search of Carlos and Kelsey. The pair had been sitting at the bar talking like old friends. It was nice to see the easy smile on Kelsey's face, and Sophie had silently applauded Carlos for bringing it out of her. She'd told Kelsey she was calling it a night, to which her friend replied that she'd like to stay out for a bit longer.

Getting out of bed, Sophie cautiously poked her head into the living room. A small gasp left her mouth at the sight of Kelsey in a robe walking Carlos to the door. Carlos turned around, looking for the source of the sound, his eyes landing on Sophie.

"Shortcake! I was hoping I'd see you this morning." He grinned. "How'd you sleep? Muscles a little sore from last night? I'm pretty sure half of the bar heard you in that supply closet. I briefly considered charging for listening privileges. Could've made a damn fortune."

Sophie opened her mouth and just as quickly closed it, looking accusingly to Kelsey who had turned her head into her shoulder and was trying to stifle the sounds of her laughter. Sophie took one last look at the pair, shook her head, and closed the door to her bedroom. She clearly wasn't ready to get out of bed yet. She crawled back under the covers, pulling them over her head, and tried like hell to erase the visual of Kelsey and Carlos together from her mind.

CHAPTER NINE

RAFE HATED FESTIVAL WEEKENDS. The twelve-hour shifts were a pain in the ass, and something about the atmosphere made people downright stupid. The thing he hated the most about festival weekends, however, was the heat. The temperatures had been in the high nineties all three days and though officers in Houston were permitted to wear short-sleeved uniforms and shorts, Rafe refused. Nothing about shorts screamed, "Respect me as an officer." Of course, Carlos happily wore the damn shorts, bragging all weekend about how much more comfortable he was than Rafe.

In the back of his mind, Rafe had spent the last three days going over Thursday night in excruciating detail. He still didn't know what had come over him. When Sophie had walked up to Rafe and slapped him, the fire in her eyes did something to him, and the little summer dress she'd been wearing set his blood boiling.

She'd been right to smack the shit out of him; he'd been an insufferable ass. The Easter comment had been one step too far, and he'd been planning to apologize to her the next time they spoke. The moment he'd seen her in that dress, all thoughts of apologizing fled his mind, a singular thought taking over: *how quickly can I get inside her?*

Rationality had left the building and he'd turned into a caveman, taking her hand without a word and having the best sex of his life in a damn storage closet of a bar. When they'd finished, she had cut him off before he could apologize again. Rafe still wasn't willing to talk about his past, but he could certainly be more cooperative than he had been.

Unfortunately, Sophie had left the bar before he could catch her, and he was no longer sure how to proceed. Rafe wasn't great with words—he didn't always say or do the right things, but he wanted to make this better. Sophie was right—she was just trying to do her job, and he was making it as difficult as he possibly could. He'd considered calling the *Houston Reporter* to request her number, but thought that might come across a little stalkerish. He'd just talk to her tonight during their ride-along. He would answer her questions, while kindly steering the conversation away from his past.

Plan in place, Rafe went about his day as he always did. He ran to the gym, worked out, and grabbed a dark roast coffee on the way home. He spent the next few hours cleaning his apartment, and before he knew it, it was time to go to work.

He pulled into the precinct parking lot, searching for and failing to find Sophie's car. He assumed she was running behind, but when he came out of the locker room, she was nowhere to be found. He spotted his partner lingering at the reception desk, and walked over to see what was going on.

"Ramirez," he barked, frustration making his tone

harsher than he'd intended. "Where the hell is Sophie? Shouldn't she be here by now?"

Carlos scratched the back of his neck, looking uncomfortable for the first time in Rafe's recent memory. "Oh, well Cap said she called this morning. Something about food poisoning or some shit." He dropped his voice to a near whisper, "Are you that bad in bed, man? Ten minutes with you and the girl is bailing on the job? Doesn't bode well."

Rafe glared at Ramirez before stomping off. At least without Sophie around he'd get his patrol car back. With a cage in the back he'd be able to make some arrests tonight. Maybe putting some criminals away would improve upon his suddenly dour mood.

"So what did you do to piss her off, Rafe?" Ramirez asked an hour into their patrol. A couple of routine traffic stops had not improved Rafe's mood; he had hardly spoken two words since leaving the station.

"Nothing," he muttered.

"Maybe she's avoiding you because you banged her in a fucking supply closet. I mean, shit, at least when I did the dirty with her roommate it was on a *bed*. I'm not a goddamn caveman."

Rafe pulled into the nearest parking lot at that. "Wait, did you say her roommate? You fucked her roommate? Carlos, are you telling me that you know where she lives?"

Carlos shifted a little in his seat. "Well, yeah? I guess so."

"You fucking guess so? You either know or you don't know. Which is it, asshole?"

His partner sighed heavily. "I know where she lives, man. But I'm not taking you there. It's like an invasion of privacy or some shit. If she wants to avoid your ass, let her."

"Do you want me to tell the guys on the force about the incident at the rodeo cook-off?"

"Woooow, that's a low blow, man. I swear, you get lost one time at the rodeo and you never live it down."

Rafe chuckled. "Hey, getting lost at the rodeo happens. But having to have them call your best friend over the speakers to come pick you up from will call? There are toddlers out there who would be embarrassed over that. You're a thirty-year-old man."

"The layout of the carnival grounds is confusing! And you know I lost my cell phone. How the hell else was I supposed to find you? You were my ride home, dude!"

"You didn't have to wander off in the first place. If you hadn't gone in search of funnel cake, none of it would've happened."

"Well, who the fuck doesn't like funnel cake?!" Ramirez exclaimed, throwing his hands in the air before shifting in his seat to look at Rafe. "Wait! Did you just call me your best friend? You did, didn't you? Awwww, Rafey, I love you too!"

Rafe scowled, pulling the patrol car back onto the street. "Oh fuck off, it's only because you're around so much. You're a proximity best friend. Now are you gonna tell me how to get to Sophie's place?"

"Fine, anything for my best friend."

Carlos directed Rafe to a small one-story house in the Heights. He was inexplicably pleased to note that her home wasn't at all far from his. The building was an older house, with a small wraparound porch. It was painted a simple robin's egg blue and had a well-maintained yard. Rafe grinned when he spotted Sophie's car in the driveway. At least she hadn't lied about being home. He parked the cruiser on the street and stepped out of the car, telling Carlos he would be just a few minutes.

"Aw, man. Are you really gonna leave me in the car?" Carlos whined.

Rafe didn't dignify his question with a response, closing the car door and approaching Sophie's house. As he walked he tried to think about what he would say to her. If she really was avoiding him because of their shared time in the supply closet, he had an easy fix for that. He could take her out on a date. Of course he wanted to see her naked again, but he'd be just as happy sitting across from her at a dinner table. He wanted to learn more about her, see her head thrown back as she laughed unguardedly; he wanted to see the teasing glint in her eyes when she said something just to rile him up. The closer he got to the door, the more sure he became. He would ask her on a date. Maybe then he could explain to her what it was about his past that he didn't want in the papers. Surely she'd understand, and maybe she'd grant him a little more time to explore the delectable body he knew she was hiding under those dressy clothes.

He knocked on the door, wincing as he realized that he had used his "cop knock." He wasn't trying to scare her, so that amount of force might not have been entirely necessary. It wasn't until he heard shuffling on the other side of the door that he remembered that if he really was here to check on a sick person, he would've brought soup or tissues —*anything really*. Before he could sprint back to his car and head to the store to remedy his social faux pas, the door was opening.

Sophie looked up at him with bright green eyes, her lips tipped down in displeasure. She looked both confused and unhappy at his arrival. Her long, blonde locks were pulled into a bun on top of her head, and she was wearing a baggy Astros T-shirt over yoga pants. Her feet were bare, toenails tipped with pretty pink polish.

"Mr. Pierce, I called the station this morning. I'm not feeling well and can't make it for the ride-along. Didn't your captain pass along the message?" she asked, crossing her arms over her chest.

Rafe shuffled his feet and cleared his throat. "Yeah, he told us that you were sick. I just wanted to, uh, check on you. I also wanted to apologize for what I said to you the other night. It was uncalled for. I know you work hard, and I respect that."

Sophie's mouth parted, her lips forming a small "o" of surprise. "Well, thank you for that. I'm sure I'll be feeling fine tomorrow, so I'll see you at five." She moved to close the door in his face, and he thrust his hand out to stop her.

"Sophie, wait. I also wanted to make sure that you weren't avoiding me after Thursday. What happened in the supply closet was—"

She cut him off before he could finish, nodding her head as she continued his sentence. "A mistake, definitely. Like I said, it can't ever happen again. I mean, can you imagine us together? We would be a train wreck. It's not like I would date a guy like you anyway. Let's just pretend it never happened."

Rafe could feel the hurt building up in his chest, and he fought for calm, willing her to clarify before he lost his temper again. "A guy like me?" he asked tentatively.

"Yeah, you know, a pretty boy. You've got this—" She gestured to his face. "—whole thing going on. I've dated guys like you before. I don't think either of us wants to make that mistake. We traded some alright orgasms. Let's call it good and part as acquaintances."

Rafe could feel his brow furrowing. "Alright orgasms? *Alright*? That's the word that you're using to describe them?"

Sophie shrugged. "Yeah, I guess so."

"Right, well. Glad you're feeling better. I guess I'll see you around." Rafe turned to walk away, salvaging what was left of his dignity.

It's not like I would date a guy like you…

He heard Sophie's door click softly behind him as he headed toward the car, her words playing on a loop in his mind.

CHAPTER TEN

OVER THE COURSE of the next few weeks, Sophie managed to find some semblance of peace with Rafe. She had completed her two weeks' worth of ride-alongs with him and Carlos, and while Rafe still wasn't the most forthcoming, he finally answered all of her questions with actual sentences. She had already written three of the four feature pieces she had planned, and was wrapping up the final one this evening. Kelsey and James were having dinner with Kelsey's parents tonight, so she was on her own.

When her stomach rumbled loud enough to wake the neighbors, she set aside her laptop and called her favorite Jewish deli to place an order for pickup. A Reuben sandwich sounded like just the thing. When the to-go server ensured her that her meal would be ready in fifteen to twenty minutes, she threw on some flip-flops, grabbed her purse, and headed to the restaurant. She hadn't really eaten much all day; her stomach had been a little too sensitive.

Fifteen minutes later, she walked into the restaurant and

headed to the to-go stand. She had almost made it there when she spotted Carlos and Rafe in a booth near the kitchen. Carlos was waving happily, and she smiled at him before heading over to say hello.

"Hey, shortcake. Looking fine, as always."

Sophie laughed and looked down at her sweatpants and wife-beater combo. "Whatever you say, Carlos."

She felt the need to steel herself before meeting Rafe's eyes. Though they had managed to work together for the last couple weeks, there was an aloofness about him that she had been unable to shake. She had lied to him that night at her house; the orgasm he'd given her was more than alright. It was the best she'd ever had. Multiple sessions with her vibrator had proven that even she wasn't capable of getting herself off that powerfully. But as much as she wanted a repeat, she knew better. She would have great sex with him for a few months, would start to fall for him, and he would get bored. He'd either end it with her or he'd cheat. It was just the way that things worked with men who looked like him, and she refused to set herself up for more heartbreak.

He met her gaze briefly, heat flaring before he lowered his lashes, hiding those gorgeous blue eyes from her.

"So, um, are y'all on your dinner break or something?"

"Yep," Carlos replied, popping the "p" at the end of the word. "This place has the best smoked salmon sandwich in the city. I make Rafe treat me at least once a week."

Sophie snorted and turned to leave. She was still starving and had a lot of work left to do tonight. Before she could walk away, the server came over to the booth with two plates of food. One whiff of the salmon sandwich on Carlos's plate had her stomach lurching. She covered her mouth as she heaved, trying to keep the vomit from coming up.

Knowing she wouldn't make it to the restroom in time, Sophie did the only thing she could do. She opened her purse, turned her back on Rafe and Carlos, and vomited the contents of her stomach into her leather Kate Spade tote.

CHAPTER ELEVEN

RAFE IMMEDIATELY JUMPED UP, rubbing Sophie's back in small circles as she purged the contents of her stomach. When it seemed she had finally finished, she straightened up and wiped her mouth, looking sheepishly at Rafe.

"I think I'll go to the bathroom and try to salvage my purse. Excuse me," she said, her cheeks flushing prettily as she turned in the direction of the restrooms. Rafe turned to Carlos, who was wearing a shocked expression, looking from his sandwich, to Sophie's retreating back, and then to Rafe.

"Hey man, I'm gonna go pay for her dinner. I doubt she will want to pull her wallet out of that mess. I'll be right back."

He walked over to the to-go stand, paid for Sophie's order, and returned to his table with the bag. Plopping himself down in the vinyl booth, he looked up at Carlos. His partner was still wearing a shocked expression, once again glancing from his sandwich to the bathroom door.

"Guess she got food poisoning again." Rafe shrugged. "She should really watch where she eats."

Carlos gaped. "You're fucking with me, right? Rafe, I bet she's pregnant. I've had food poisoning, and the scent of a sandwich has never caused me to throw up. When my sister was pregnant, though, fish made her sick constantly. We couldn't even have it in the house when she came over."

Rafe shook his head. "We had sex a couple of weeks ago. That's way too soon for morning sickness, dude. Besides, we used a condom."

Even as his said this, he pulled his smart phone out of his pocket and searched morning sickness. His stomach dropped as the search results populated.

"Well?" Carlos asked impatiently.

Rafe looked up at his friend and back down to his phone, reading out loud, "'Though most women experience morning sickness after six weeks of pregnancy, it can start as early as the fourth week.' No, it isn't possible. Carlos, it hasn't been four weeks. Pull up the calendar on your phone."

Carlos was counting on his hand, ticking back the days, trying to calculate the number of weeks it had been since Rafe and Sophie had had sex at the bar. "Carlos! Stop fucking around and pull out your phone! It was the week before the music festival, remember?"

His friend pulled out his cell phone, consulting the calendar app, as Rafe read and re-read the information on his screen.

"Rafe…" Carlos said quietly. "It'll have been four weeks tomorrow."

Sophie chose that moment to return from the bathroom. "I am so sorry about that, you guys." She smiled ruefully at them. "Hopefully I didn't ruin your appetite. I'll just go grab my dinner and head home."

Rafe, never the best at finesse, blurted out the first thing that came to mind. "Sophie, when was the last time you got your period?"

"WHAT? How the hell is that any of your business?"

"It's just, you smelled the fish and then you threw up, and it's been four weeks, and Google says that four weeks is a feasible length of time. So I was thinking, that maybe if you haven't gotten your period, it could be possible...you could be..." Rafe took a deep breath. His mind was a mess.

Pregnant? She can't be pregnant. It just isn't possible. She wouldn't even go on a date with me, and now she could be having my kid?

He didn't know what to say anymore. Pushing his plate aside, he rested his forehead on the table with a *thunk*.

Carlos apologized and explained that they had paid for her food. He heard Sophie say goodbye, her footsteps echoing on the tile as she left the restaurant. Rafe was still trying to get his breathing under control when he felt Carlos poke him with a fork.

"Hey bestie, you alive over there?"

Rafe grunted, lifting his head a few inches and thunking it back down onto the table.

"You need to talk to her, find a way to get her to take a test. If she's pregnant, you'll have to figure some shit out."

Rafe lifted his head. He could feel his mouth gaping but was unable to push out any words. Carlos signaled for the check and pulled out his wallet.

"I guess this one can be on me. You have a college tuition to save up for now, buddy."

Rafe felt a strangled sound leave his throat before his forehead hit the table again.

"First Response, EPT, Clearblue—how the fuck are you supposed to pick one?" Carlos asked Rafe, picking up each box in turn and examining it before returning it to the shelf. "There should just be one test. I bet I could make a fortune marketing a pregnancy test for men to buy. I can see it now: the girl pees on the stick and the little box says 'Fucked' or 'Not Fucked.' 'Not Fucked,' of course, meaning not pregnant."

Rafe heaved a sigh and rubbed his hand along the back of his neck. He lifted his basket to the shelf and, one by one, tipped the three major pregnancy test brands into it. He was turning to leave the aisle when Carlos added something to the basket.

"A twenty-four pack of condoms, Carlos? Really? Now is not the time to be funny."

"Whoa, who said anything about being funny? Consider them a present from you to me for helping out with this shit. I'm the one who called the captain and explained the situation. He didn't chew *your* ass out for asking for the rest of the night off; he chewed out mine. Besides, I need as many of those damn things as I can get now. I'll be double wrapping for months. No way I'm getting myself into a mess like this."

"Really," Rafe said drily. "You aren't joking? Then why'd

you get Magnums, dude? I highly doubt you're packing that much heat."

"Ohhh you wanna compare? Have a little sword fight in the aisle of the drugstore? I'll show you mine if you show me yours, Officer."

Despite his situation, Rafe laughed, slapping his friend on the arm as he walked toward the front of the store. "Alright, Casanova, calm down. Let's get the hell out of here."

CHAPTER TWELVE

SOPHIE HAD FINISHED her dinner and was watching *The Greatest Showman* on the couch when she heard Kelsey come in through the front door.

"Hey roomie, I'm home!" Kelsey shouted, walking into the living room and plopping down next to her. "Whoa, are you watching our movie without me? You bitch! I thought we were friends!"

Sophie paused the movie and shrugged. "It's not my fault your ass took forever eating dinner with the family."

Kelsey huffed and pushed up off the couch. "Well, James zonked out at my parents' house so he's gonna stay there tonight. I'll pick him up in the morning. In the meantime, how about we open a bottle of wine and celebrate Zac Efron, the finest ass in show business."

Sophie laughed, starting the movie back up as Kelsey walked into the kitchen to grab a bottle and a couple glasses. Hugh Jackman was just about to proposition Zac Efron when she heard a knock at the door. She paused the movie again and went to see who was disrupting her movie night.

Looking through the peephole, she took in Rafe's nervous face. He looked like he was about to have a damn panic attack.

She threw open the door and Rafe brushed past her, holding a drugstore bag, a smirking Carlos in tow. "Sophie, we need to talk," he started, pacing in the entry of her house.

"Sure," she mumbled. "Come right in."

Carlos whistled. "Nice digs you got here, shortcake. I meant to tell you before, but I was a little…distracted."

"Um, thanks, Carlos. Rafe, what the hell is going on?"

Rafe took a deep breath, pushed it back out, and ran his fingers through his hair before shoving his hands in his pockets.

"You're pregnant," he muttered, looking up and meeting her eyes.

"Umm, no?"

"You are, though!" he exclaimed. "Carlos said that his sister used to throw up when she smelled fish, and morning sickness can start as early as four weeks into a pregnancy, and we had sex almost exactly four weeks ago. Are your breasts bigger? I think they look a little bigger too. Isn't that a sign of pregnancy?"

Rafe went back to furiously pacing, running his fingers through his hair again, the drugstore bag forgotten at his feet.

"Rafe, I'm not pregnant. We used a condom. I've just been feeling queasy all day. I'm sure it's nothing. I have a sensitive stomach, that's all."

Carlos, who had been looking through the assorted items on the small table in the entryway, plucked the bag up off the floor and handed it to her.

"Well, we got you these. Just, you know, to be sure."

She looked in the bag and pulled out the first item she saw. "Condoms? A twenty-four pack of Magnum condoms? Why do I need these?"

Carlos grinned sheepishly, snatching the condoms out of her hand and trying, unsuccessfully, to hide them in his pocket. "Sorry, those are mine."

"Magnums, huh? Damn, good for Kelsey." She peered into the bag, seeing an assortment of pregnancy tests.

"So you want me to take these, Rafe? Will that make you feel better?"

Rafe simply nodded, still pacing furiously and looking at the floor. Kelsey walked into the entry, holding two glasses of wine and wearing a very confused expression. She handed one glass to Sophie and took a big sip before addressing the room.

"Somebody wanna tell me why pretty boy over here looks like he's about to ralph all over the carpet?"

Sophie scoffed. "Rafe is under the impression I'm pregnant." She lifted the wine glass to her lips and managed one tiny sip before Rafe snatched it out of her hands.

"Are you fucking crazy? You can't drink if you're pregnant!" He looked at the glass for a moment and downed it in three quick gulps. He then reached over, took Kelsey's glass out of her hands, and downed it too. "No wine until I see the test results," he grumbled.

"Hey jackass! I'm not the pregnant one! Why the hell did you have to take my wine?"

Rafe shrugged. "I needed it more than you did."

Kelsey stomped off toward the kitchen with her now-empty glass, presumably in search of more wine. Carlos looked between Rafe and Sophie before shrugging and following her.

"Fine, I'll take a damn test. Just give me a minute, okay?"

Sophie walked through the living room to her bedroom. She padded into the en-suite bathroom, Rafe following her every step of the way.

"Do you think I'm going to let you watch me pee?" she asked rhetorically, shooing Rafe out of the bathroom and closing the door in his face. She took a deep breath and pulled out the first box in the bag. Opening the box, she unwrapped a pregnancy test and squatted uncomfortably over the toilet to do her business.

"This would've been a lot easier to do with some wine in my system, ya know!" she shouted at the door.

She peed on the stick and set it on the counter. The box said she would know in three minutes, so she set a timer on her phone and calmly waited for the results. She knew the test would be negative; she'd gotten her period a couple of weeks ago, hadn't she? She looked at the unopened box of tampons sitting on her counter. Counting back on her hands, she did some fast period math and realized that she hadn't had her period since before she and Rafe had had sex. She was almost two weeks late.

She had just begun to panic when the timer went off on her phone, alerting her to the end of the three minutes. Sophie took a steadying breath and looked down at the test. The small word was light in color but clearly visible: POSITIVE.

"SHIT!"

CHAPTER THIRTEEN

RAFE HEARD Sophie's exclamation through the door and immediately stopped pacing, sinking to the floor. He put his head in his hands and tried to hold the panic at bay. He'd always wanted to be a father, but it was too soon. When he'd imagined this moment home alone in bed, he'd always thought he'd be in that bathroom with her. He and his imaginary wife would see the positive sign on the pregnancy test and he'd wrap her in a huge hug. He'd always known he would cry the day he found out he was going to be a father, but he never thought it would be alone on a bedroom floor while his one-night stand took a test in the next room.

He was positive he'd make a great dad; he was already half in love with the tiny peanut growing in Sophie's uterus. What kind of life could he have with his child, though? He'd never imagined a joint-custody situation. He wanted to wake up every morning knowing that his child was asleep in the next room. Sophie wouldn't even consider dating him, much less living in the same house as him.

He heard the bathroom door open quietly and felt more

than saw Sophie sit down on the floor next to him. He looked up at her and saw that she was staring at the test clutched in her hands. Reaching over, he plucked it from her fingers, his hand shaking as he pulled it toward him. The word *positive* was clear on the small piece of plastic.

In that moment, he couldn't hold back the smile that broke over his face. He was going to be a father. Sure, the situation wasn't ideal, but he was so excited to hold his child in his arms. He hadn't had a real childhood, bouncing from foster home to foster home until the age of eighteen. He would give this child *everything*. His baby had just become the center of his universe, and there was no going back.

He was broken from his thoughts by Sophie's voice. "Rafe, what the hell are we going to do?"

Rafe looked up at her, confused. "What option do we have? We're going to have this baby, and we're going to raise it."

Sophie's face fell. "I'm not ready to be a mom yet. We don't even like each other. How could we possibly raise a child together?"

Rafe wrapped an arm around her, pulling her into his side. "We'll figure it out as we go. Plus, we have nine months to plan. Who knows, maybe you'll stop hating me in that time."

Sophie laughed. "Maybe if you'd stop being a high-handed ass, I'd stop hating you."

"I hate to break it to you, but high-handed is the only packaging this toy comes in."

Rafe stood, offering Sophie his hands and pulling her up with him. He wrapped his arms around her waist and pulled her in for a hug. He leaned his forehead against hers and took a deep breath. "We can do this, Soph. I know we can."

She pulled back, looking into his eyes as though trying to gauge the sincerity in his words. "What makes you so certain? The only thing I know for sure is that I have no idea how to be a parent." She pulled out of his arms and looked up at him.

"I know this is huge, Sophie. *Trust me*, I know that. I also know that I've wanted this my entire life. I want this child with every part of my being. I have no fucking clue how to raise a kid, but do you really think that anyone does? The best thing that we can do is prepare and love our baby with everything that we have."

Though she wasn't nearly as confident as he was, Sophie nodded.

Everything worth having in life is at least a little terrifying, right?

"I can't say that I don't still have my doubts, Rafe. This is not how I expected for things to go. There is no guarantee that I won't freak out a few times over the next few months, but knowing that I'm not in this alone makes my choice a little easier."

Rafe pulled Sophie back to him and kissed her on the forehead. "No," he murmured softly against her skin. "You're definitely not alone."

Leaving the comfort of her bedroom Sophie pulled Rafe into the living room, where Carlos and Kelsey had resumed *The Greatest Showman*.

"Okay, so this dude is PT Barnum? Why is he singing? I'm pretty sure Barnum didn't sing in real life."

Kelsey let out an exasperated groan. "Just watch the fucking movie, Carlos."

Sophie cleared her throat and the pair of them whipped around to look at her, the movie forgotten. Rafe did his best to keep his expression as ambiguous as possible. He wasn't sure Sophie was ready to tell their friends yet, so he decided to let her take the lead.

Carlos, ever the impatient member of their group was the first to speak. "Well? What did the test say?"

Sophie took a calming breath, reaching for Rafe's hand. "It was positive," she said quietly.

Carlos immediately jumped off the couch, whooping loudly. "We're going to have a baby!" He grabbed Rafe, wrapping him in a massive hug. Sophie had released his hand and was speaking to Kelsey in quiet tones on the couch. He cleared his throat when Carlos's hug passed the thirty-second mark.

"Alright, man. You can let go now."

Carlos grunted and released Rafe with an awkward pat on the back. "I mean, congratulations, man," he said, deepening his voice. "I need a beer and a stogie; this shit is too emotional for my tastes."

Sophie looked up from her conversation with Kelsey. "I think I need to get some rest. Rafe, I'll schedule a doctor's appointment and text you the time and place."

Rafe rubbed his chin, a little uncomfortable. "I guess I should get your number now, huh?"

At this, Carlos burst out laughing. He doubled over, cackling gleefully. When he finally managed to compose himself, he straightened and wiped imaginary tears from his eyes. "Oh man, you got her pregnant and don't even have her phone number. Pretty boy, that is fucking priceless."

CHAPTER FOURTEEN

BEFORE SOPHIE WENT to bed that night, she texted her boss and took a personal day. If she was going to do this, she needed to go to a doctor. Kelsey had told her she'd need to cut caffeine out of her diet completely and go on prenatal vitamins. Was she really considering doing this? She hadn't really given much thought to being a parent; she'd always kind of assumed that she would eventually meet the right guy, fall in love, and start a family. Until now, that future had been entirely theoretical. It had always been something that would happen eventually, once her career was established, once she'd left the *Houston Reporter* and had begun working for a publishing house.

There was so much to think about if she was going to proceed with this pregnancy. She was close to getting a recommendation letter from her boss; she could feel it. What impact would this baby have on her possible career? Rafe's job was in Houston, and she was planning to move to New York sometime within the next year. Considering how excited he was to be a father, could she really take this child away from him?

Sophie was hit with a sudden wave of resentment, not for the fetus growing within her, but for the situation she found herself in. She couldn't stay in Houston; it had never been a part of her plan. Sophie had never been the type of woman to throw her dreams away for a man, and she couldn't start now. This baby was like a chain, shackling her to Rafe and to this city she was so ready to leave. Even as she had the thought, she hated herself for it, and just like that the doubt crept in.

What if I'm too selfish to be a parent?

Though she was terrified, she knew that abortion wasn't an option for her. Sophie had always been of the belief that a woman could do with her body what she wished. Though she understood why other women had abortions, and would never begrudge them their choice, she knew that she would never be able to go through with the procedure herself. From the moment she'd seen the positive test result, she'd felt a connection to the child growing inside of her. Under the comforter, she moved her hand down to her stomach. She wouldn't start to show for a few more months, but something had changed in her. She could feel her baby there, and she already loved it. She fell asleep that night with tears on her cheeks and her hand on her stomach.

She woke up in the morning to the chime of a text notification. Sophie rolled over and grabbed her phone off of the nightstand, rubbing her bleary eyes to clear her vision. It was only seven-thirteen, but she already had a text from a clearly excited Rafe.

Rafe: I found an app I think you would like. It's

called Ovia, and it shows you the size of the baby, and tells you what to expect during this time in your pregnancy and how your body is changing.

Rafe: Did you know that our baby is the size of a poppy seed right now?

Sophie smiled at his enthusiasm, feeling just a little bit more sure about their decision. She still didn't know how all of this was going to play out, but she knew that he would be there with her every step of the way.

Sophie: You're so weird.

Sophie: ...I'll download it.

After a shower and a cup of decaf tea, Sophie called her gynecologist's office and scheduled an appointment. Due to a last-minute cancellation, she was lucky enough to get a spot today. She immediately texted Rafe with the address and time before grabbing her purse and heading out the door. She was halfway to her car when she realized that her appointment was at eleven a.m. and it was still only eight.

Sighing and shaking her head at her own stupidity, Sophie walked back into her house and plopped down on the couch. She downloaded Ovia from the app store, thinking she might as well check out the app Rafe was so excited about. Two minutes into setup, she was already frustrated. How the hell was she supposed to know when her due date was? She hadn't even been to the doctor yet!

Sophie: This app is stupid. I can't know my due date if I haven't seen a doctor yet.

Rafe: LOL, I calculated the due date to be somewhere around March 14th.

Sophie: Overachiever.

She typed in the due date Rafe had calculated and found out that her baby's first placental cells were currently developing. She had no idea what any of that meant, and found herself getting frustrated all over again. Feeling wholly unprepared to deal with the things going on in her body, she grabbed her purse and headed to her local bookstore. Bookstores held all of the answers.

Walking into a bookstore was like coming home for Sophie. Nothing could quite compare to the smell of fresh books and fresher coffee. Unfortunately, she could only indulge in one of those, so she headed to the young adult section. If she was going to buy pregnancy books, she would have to work up to it. She grabbed the latest Jenn Bennett book off of the shelf, and treated herself to a few others while she was at it. She then headed over to the kids section, picking up a few of her favorite children's books for James. Her godson would be a reader if it killed her.

After she had procrastinated for about an hour, Sophie looked around, making sure she knew nobody in the store, before creeping over to the parenting section.

Holy shit, there are so many choices.

The aisle was jam-packed with colorful books, celebrity guides to parenting (pass), books on child-raising theory, and finally, a pregnancy section. She quickly grabbed *What to*

Expect When You're Expecting, a classic, and a copy of *Mayo Clinic Guide to a Healthy Pregnancy*. She was about to leave the aisle when she spotted a book called *The Birth Partner*. She threw it on top of her pile of books, figuring that Rafe would plow through it and any other pregnancy book she offered him.

On her way to the register, Sophie shuffled around her books, hiding the pregnancy books at the bottom of the pile, as though that would hide them from the checkout clerk. When it was her turn in line, the person behind the counter efficiently scanned and packed her items before asking if she had a membership card.

Sophie scoffed. She practically lived here; of course she had one. Only amateurs were dumb enough not to take advantage of that ten percent discount.

By the time she'd gotten back in her car, she had thirty minutes to make it to her gynecologist's office. Fortunately, traffic was light on a Thursday morning, and she pulled into the clinic parking lot with ten minutes to spare. Before she could even step out of her car, Rafe was there, pulling the door open farther and offering a hand to help her stand.

"I'm not showing yet. I can get out of a car just fine by myself, thank you."

Rafe smiled and shrugged. "Can't fault a man for trying to be chivalrous."

She closed the door behind her and locked the car. Throwing her keys back in her purse, she glanced at Rafe, taking in his appearance. His blonde hair was still wet, as though he'd just stepped out of the shower, and he was wearing his usual: a pair of dark-wash jeans and a Henley. What must his closet look like? Sophie guessed it was filled to the brim with this exact outfit in variations of gray, blue, and black. A five o'clock shadow graced his jawline, making her want to nibble on it just a little bit. The man looked entirely too fuckable for his own good, and Sophie had to remind herself that looking at him this way had gotten her into her current predicament.

She pivoted and walked toward the front door of the doctor's office, leaving Rafe behind. Unfortunately, his legs were much longer and he quickly caught up, thrusting a to-go cup of something in front of her.

"Coffee? You brought me coffee?"

"Well, I did some research online, and most doctors say that one cup a day won't hurt you or the baby. Plus, I know you practically live on the stuff, and I remembered your order from the last time we ran into each other at the coffee shop." He shrugged.

Sophie took a deep drink from the coffee cup, moaning loudly as she felt the warm drink slide down her throat. She closed her eyes, savoring the taste. When she opened them, Rafe was grinning widely at her. She watched as he reached down, adjusting the rapidly growing situation in his pants.

"Sounds like that coffee gives better orgasms than I do," he said with a chuckle.

"Don't be offended. If I had to choose between a life of celibacy and a life without coffee, I would drop sex so fast it would make your head spin. Sign me up to be a nun and keep the cappuccinos coming."

Rafe barked out a surprised laugh, his eyes moving to her lips. The heat she was becoming all too familiar with had returned to his eyes. He leaned down slowly, making his intent clear, and swiped his tongue across her bottom lip. He kissed her gently before pulling back.

"You had a little foam on your lip," he said, turning away

from her and walking into the building. Sophie followed him, her legs feeling a little bit weaker than they had just a few moments ago.

After she'd checked in with reception and taken a seat in the waiting room, she pulled her phone out of her purse and texted Kelsey. She needed reinforcements.

Sophie: He brought me coffee…

Kelsey: Marry him. Wait, who brought you coffee?

Kelsey: Actually, doesn't matter. Same answer. Put a ring on that shit.

Sophie: Rafe did. He showed up to the doctor's appointment, brought me a bone-dry cappuccino, and then kissed me in the parking lot.

Kelsey: Are you still at the doctor's office? The guy deserves at least a thank you BJ. Reschedule and thank the man properly.

Sophie: Just because I'm having a baby with him doesn't mean I want to start anything, Kels! When do pregnancy hormones start making you horny? I'm pretty sure that's what's going on.

Kelsey: Yeahhh, nice try. That happens in your second trimester. You're just plain horny now.

Sophie: Well, fuck me.

Kelsey: Say that to him and you're golden.

Sophie chuckled, tucking her phone back into her purse. She should've known Kelsey would have no helpful response. Give the woman coffee and you were in the running for a Nobel Prize.

"What's so funny?" Rafe asked, smiling softly at her. Sophie wasn't sure what to do with this new Rafe. She was used to quiet, sullen, asshole Rafe. This new version of him was disconcerting. She had been attracted to him before— when he was a player and an all-around dick. She had a feeling that this version of Rafe—the open and honest one— could steal her heart. They were having a baby together, but the last thing Sophie wanted was to fall for him. She'd been heartbroken enough times in her past to know that men who looked like him were trouble.

"Oh…" Sophie answered distractedly. "Just Kelsey being a dork. She thinks that you deserve a blow job for bringing me coffee."

Rafe made a choking sound and started coughing. He gestured at his throat and mumbled, "Went down the wrong pipe."

Sophie blushed. She hadn't meant to let that slip, but her mind was elsewhere, and it had just sort of popped out. She'd never been the best at filtering her thoughts.

Once Rafe had recovered, he offered her a boyish grin and shrugged. "I mean, I wouldn't be opposed to that form of gratitude."

Unbidden, an image of her on her knees in front of Rafe, taking him into her mouth, filled her mind. She shifted in her seat and felt herself flush. Before she could come up with some sort of response, a nurse came into the waiting room and called her name.

Rafe started to get up, but Sophie waved him back. "No, no, you can wait here. I'll let you know what the doctor says."

He shot her a dark look and stood. "If you think I'm missing a second of this, you're fucking crazy."

CHAPTER FIFTEEN

THE DOCTOR'S appointment had gone well. Sophie's gynecologist was also a licensed OB/GYN, so they wouldn't have to find another doctor to get her through the pregnancy. Dr. Welsh had given Sophie a urine pregnancy test, something about detecting a change in her hCG levels. They would have the results of the test by Monday, but he had assured them that if the at-home test had said she was pregnant, this test wouldn't change anything. The change in hCG levels would let them know if the pregnancy was healthy. Since they knew the exact date of conception, and the date of Sophie's last period, he was also able to tell them that the estimated due date would be around the tenth of March.

He gave Sophie a list of do's and don'ts and told them that they would receive a call by Monday afternoon to confirm that the pregnancy wasn't chemical or ectopic. From there, they would schedule an appointment at the ten-week mark for the baby's first ultrasound. He had also recommended a prenatal vitamin and a few parenting books.

Now, more than ever, Rafe wanted to spend more time with Sophie. It wasn't just that she was the mother of his child, it was everything about her. Her dry wit and coffee addiction, the way she spoke with her whole body, gesturing wildly as she told stories. He knew though that she wasn't ready for that and that he needed to bide his time.

"So I've been thinking..." he said cautiously. "Maybe we should get to know each other better. We are having a baby together, so it might be good to at least know the basic shit. I don't even know your birthday."

Sophie laughed. "It's September sixteenth. Getting to know you better sounds good, but I still won't date you."

Rafe clutched his heart dramatically. "You wound me. Here I was, planning our wedding and naming our four other children."

She smacked him lightly on the arm. "Don't be a drama queen. You're spending way too much time with Carlos."

He really had been spending too much time with his partner. He'd caught himself saying "that's what she said" the other day at work. It hadn't been a proud moment.

Before he left, Rafe and Sophie had agreed to spend some time getting to know one another over the next few weeks. She'd also given him a parenting book, a gesture that had made him smile. He didn't have the heart to tell her that he already owned it. He'd gone a little crazy on Amazon the previous night, purchasing ten pregnancy books and five parenting ones.

Rafe was grateful for the next two days off; he and Carlos had traded with another patrol team. This morning before the doctor's appointment, he had gone to his apartment's leasing office and requested to move to a two-bedroom apartment. He'd have to pay one month's rent at both places, but a small dip into his savings account wouldn't hurt anything. He and Carlos would be spending all of today and tomorrow moving his things to the new place. He still wasn't sure how custody with Sophie would work out, but he wanted to make sure that his child had their own room when they came along.

One day, thirty boxes, and one whiny-ass Carlos later, Rafe and all of his belongings had been successfully moved into his new apartment. Moving all of his things with only Carlos for help had been exhausting, but so worth it.

Rafe was in his bedroom unpacking his sheets and the pregnancy books when Carlos wandered in, grumbling. His friend collapsed on the floor and sprawled out, groaning like a dying man.

"Hey Carlos, help me move some boxes, you said. *It'll be fun*, you said. I am never listening to you again. You know, I honestly think I'm sore enough to forgo sex right now. I ache everywhere."

"Don't be a pussy, it wasn't that bad," Rafe replied, carefully setting the pregnancy books on his bedside table. He'd finished one last night and couldn't wait to start on the rest.

"I need to find new friends," Carlos grumbled. "You owe me like fifty beers. And some shots. Maybe a lap dance."

"I owe you one beer at the most. I've had to put up with your annoying ass for a year now. Consider this your way of thanking me for not punching you."

"You have punched me, you fucker!"

Rafe shrugged. "Well, you deserved it that time."

"How the fuck did I deserve it?"

"You took all of my clothes while I was showering at the gym and replaced them with a *leotard*, Carlos. I had to walk home in that damn thing!"

Carlos chuckled. "Yeah, those pictures were priceless. Your ass in that hot-pink leotard is the background on my phone."

"Is there something you need to tell me, man? We can get that beer at a gay bar if you want. I support your choices."

Carlos threw Rafe a glare that would send a lesser man cowering. "Fuck you. A beer is a beer though, and the gay bar on Bagby has karaoke on Friday nights."

Over the next few weeks, work was crazy for Rafe, and his erratic schedule had kept him from really getting to see Sophie. Determined to form some sort of relationship with the mother of his child, even if it was just a friendship, he'd taken to texting her. A couple of patrol teams had been transferred to another precinct, leaving his understaffed. The twelve-hour shifts he was constantly pulling were made bearable when he talked to Sophie.

SIX WEEKS PREGNANT

Rafe: Our baby's eyes are beginning to form now.

Sophie: And apparently she is the size of a blueberry.

Rafe: She? Are you assigning a gender to our child already?

Sophie: Shut up, she just feels like a girl.

Rafe: The baby is the size of a blueberry... I imagine she feels more like small fruit than anything.

Sophie: *Gasp* How dare you say such a thing about our precious little girl.

Sophie: Thanks a lot, asshole, now I'm picturing that annoying kid from Willy Wonka that turns into a blueberry.

Rafe: "Violet, you're turning violet!"

Rafe: Btw the movie is called CHARLIE and the Chocolate Factory. Not Willy Wonka...

Sophie: My child has no father.

SEVEN WEEKS PREGNANT

Sophie: So if Violet is now raspberry sized, do we need to rename her?

Rafe: Ummm...you are not naming my son Violet.

Sophie: Did you knock up some other chick? You are not getting a son. I'm determined. This baby WILL be a girl.

Rafe: What's wrong with having a boy?

Sophie: Kelsey MADE me watch James today and it was torture. That little guy is energetic and always throwing shit, and I'm exhausted.

Rafe: How long did you watch him?

Sophie: . . .

Rafe: Sophie, how long did you watch James?

Sophie: Okay, okay, it was just while she was in the shower. But it was a REALLY LONG SHOWER. And that kid is out to get me. He pelted a Cheerio right at my head. Could've taken an eye out.

Rafe: THE HORROR! Death by Cheerio! You'll need therapy for years to recover from your near-death experience.

Sophie: It was a really hard Cheerio.

Rafe: Fine, we will feed our SON soggy Cheerios.

EIGHT WEEKS PREGNANT

Sophie: I hate you.

Rafe: I know, but what did I do this time?

Sophie: YOU GOT ME PREGNANT!

Sophie: I JUST PUKED IN THE GROCERY STORE.

Rafe: Do we need to get you another replacement purse?

Sophie: Ha Ha. You're so funny. Also, yes.

Rafe: So the morning sickness is going well then?

Sophie: Oh, it's fantastic. The cravings have started setting in too. So I want to eat ice cream and pie...OMG PIE.

Sophie: I think I just came.

Rafe: Thinking about pie?

Sophie: No?

Rafe: Go get pie, Soph.

Sophie: I CAN'T. This stupid app says that I shouldn't indulge in my cravings if I want to have a healthy pregnancy.

Rafe: I didn't say you should eat a whole pie. I don't think one slice would hurt.

Sophie: But…I'm already home. If I go back to the store I could just puke again. I'll settle for drooling over Food Network bake-offs.

Rafe: Hmmm…sounds like you're just setting yourself up for disappointment.

Sophie: OMG RAFE GET OVER HERE.

Rafe: I'm working until 6 a.m. What's wrong?

Sophie: There's someone at my door...at 11 at night. And Kelsey isn't home! She's staying with her parents. GET OVER HERE!

Rafe: Answer the door, Sophie.

Sophie: Are you crazy??

Rafe: Open the damn door.

Sophie: You had pie delivered to my house?

Sophie: You're my new favorite person. I may like you enough to have your babies.

Rafe: Ha. I see what you did there.

Rafe: You're welcome.

NINE WEEKS PREGNANT

Sophie: I think the pregnancy hormones are out to get me.

Rafe: Crying over the ASPCA commercial again?

Sophie: Nooooo. . .

Sophie: There was this commercial advertising a

button that older people can push. You know, the "Help, I've fallen and can't get up" commercials?

Rafe: Oh jeez, that super cheesy one with the horrible acting? Sophie, you know the old guy didn't ACTUALLY fall down, right?

Sophie: He seemed so scared. . .

Sophie: And he was all alone, and he'd fallen and couldn't get up. It was so sad.

Rafe: I promise the guy is fine, Soph. He was just acting.

Sophie: You're positive?

Rafe: Yes, he's fine.

Sophie: Oh no. . .

Sophie: ASPCA commercial is back.

Rafe: Crying again?

Sophie: Spend all your time waiting. . .

Rafe: Don't do it, Sophie. Don't sing that damn song.

Sophie: For that second chance. . .

Rafe: Yep, you're gonna sing it anyway, aren't you?

Sophie: For a break that would make it okay...

Rafe: Yes, I know the lyrics. You texted them to me yesterday.

Sophie: IN THE ARMS OF THE ANGEL...

Rafe: I'm disconnecting your cable the next time I come over.

CHAPTER SIXTEEN

THE LAST FEW weeks had been a whirlwind for Sophie. Being pregnant was already affecting her body in ways that she hadn't expected so soon. The morning sickness had finally passed and the cravings had been brutal. She knew she needed to eat healthy, but whoever had compiled the information for this app obviously hadn't ever eaten strawberry rhubarb pie. The stuff was like crack, honestly.

On TV, pregnant women had always seemed so glowing and perfect and gorgeous. Sophie felt like a hot freaking mess. She was bloated as hell, had acne for the first time since high school (one zit counted as acne—IT DID), and she was having a hell of a time staying asleep. She would sleep for three hours at a time and then wake up. As a result, in addition to her acne, Sophie had bags under her eyes.

She'd already told her boss about her situation, wanting to be completely transparent, and had been relegated to copyediting duty only. Some would consider this a punishment, but Sophie loved copyediting. Getting to really sink into a story, check for proper grammar and punctuation, and not have to worry about coming up with witty yet informative content was her version of heaven.

She'd finished her series of features on Rafe and had gotten wonderful feedback on it. She had even done a one-article feature on Carlos, complete with a picture of him and Rafe. The women of Houston were going crazy for the partners. Some had actually tried calling the *Houston Reporter* offices for contact information, and they'd received more envelopes with panties and phone numbers stuffed into them than she'd like to admit. If they were getting all of this mail at the office, she couldn't even begin to imagine what the precinct was dealing with.

The News section had done a short piece on the impact the two men were having on the 911 dispatch center. Apparently, women were making up accidents and emergencies in an effort to see "Houston's Finest" (as the duo was now being dubbed). The *Houston Reporter* had written the article in an effort to stop the madness, but Houston's single population would not be culled so easily.

According to Rafe, Carlos was loving the attention, but every time Sophie mentioned it to Kelsey at home, her best friend had fumed and changed the subject. Sophie knew that they'd slept together at least once, but Kelsey was surprisingly tight-lipped about the whole thing, saying only that her focus was on James and finalizing her divorce.

Surprisingly, Rafe had been a huge source of comfort for Sophie thus far. He'd texted her at least once a day to check up on her and had, on numerous occasions, gotten pie delivered to her house. Though they hadn't seen one another, his texts always managed to cheer her up, and she was really starting to appreciate his friendship. If, alone in her bed at night, she found herself wishing for more, she shut the thoughts down as quickly as possible. She refused to repeat the mistakes she'd made in her past.

Today would be her first time seeing him since that initial doctor's appointment. As promised, the Monday after the appointment, the doctor had called to inform her that she was indeed pregnant and that it appeared to be a healthy pregnancy thus far. She had scheduled a follow-up appointment at ten weeks so that they could do their very first ultrasound. She wasn't showing yet, but she often found herself resting her hand on her stomach. She was terrified but excited at the same time. The more she and Rafe talked about their child, the more connected she became to the little girl. She was still adamant that she would have a girl, while Rafe was convinced they would have a boy.

When she pulled into the parking lot of her OB/GYN's office and saw Rafe's car, she felt her stomach drop, and a smile broke over her face. She tried to tell herself that she was just excited to hear her baby's heartbeat for the first time, but she knew that a part of her thrilled at the chance to see Rafe again.

As she approached the front door of the clinic, she saw Rafe pacing and speaking on his phone. She paused for a moment to take him in; he'd dressed up today, trading in the Henley and jeans for a slate gray pair of dress slacks and a light blue button-down. The sleeves of the button-down were rolled to his elbow, and the muscles in his forearm were corded, flexing as he tightened and loosened his grip on the phone. If Rafe in casual clothes was handsome, in dress clothes he was devastating. The blue of the shirt made his eyes pop, and the sleeves loosely hugged his biceps as he moved. The dress pants somehow made his legs look longer, tapering off neatly to show off a pair of black dress shoes.

"Yeah, man, the interview is today at four. I've heard Sergeant Oshiro is a hard guy to impress so I hope it goes well."

Interview? Sophie stepped closer, into Rafe's line of sight. The moment he spotted her, his entire face lit up, a gorgeous smile transforming his features.

"Carlos, I gotta go." Rafe let out a chuckle. "I'll be sure to ask her."

Another pause. "Yes, I'll call you after, Mother. Bye."

Rafe hung up the phone and walked over to wrap Sophie in a crushing hug. "Hey beautiful," he murmured into her hair.

Sophie cleared her throat and pulled back, reluctantly breaking the embrace. Before she could step away, Rafe put his hand on her stomach, resting it there for a moment before pulling back.

"I don't know why, but I thought you'd be showing by now."

"From what I've read, it won't be very obvious until the twelve-week mark, but..." She smoothed her big T-shirt over her belly. "There is a little bit of a bump. I'm sure it's mostly water weight. Let's go check in so you can tell me about this interview."

Rafe held the door open for her, his hand on the small of her back as he followed her into the waiting room. Sophie's skin fairly sizzled at the contact through her T-shirt. She fought the shiver trying to work its way up her body and checked in at reception.

Once they'd taken a seat, she turned to Rafe. "Interview?"

"Well, first of all, Carlos wanted me to make a request." Sophie motioned for him to continue, and Rafe released a heavy sigh. "If our baby is a boy, he'd like for us to name him Carlos, naturally."

Sophie scoffed and rolled her eyes. "All the more reason to hope we have a girl."

Rafe shot her a grin. "Oh no, it gets better. If we have a girl, Carlos wants us to name her Carlita."

"Carlita? Why not Carla? Is Carlita even a name?"

Rafe's lips tipped up into his trademark smirk. "I've tried explaining that to him, but he's dead set on Carlita. He's also declared himself the baby's godfather. He came into work the other day in a full suit and fedora and started spouting lines from the movie."

Sophie snorted. "You've got to be kidding me."

"If you think I'm joking you must not know Carlos well."

"Touché. Now stop stalling and tell me about this interview."

Rafe leaned back into the waiting room chair and scrubbed his hand over his face. "It's nothing really. I applied to be a detective in the homicide unit. The whole thing is a long shot because I've only been on the force for four years and they typically ask for five years' minimum experience. Sometimes, they'll count a college degree as one year though, so I have my fingers crossed."

"Oh, wow. Rafe, that's incredible! Your interview is today?"

"Yeah, and the guy interviewing me is a real hardass; he doesn't fuck around. Like I said, it isn't a huge deal. It probably won't happen anyway."

"Bullshit, it is absolutely a big deal! You wouldn't apply for the position if you didn't want it. You're not the kind of person who does anything without putting some thought into it. In fact, what was your major in college?"

Rafe rubbed the back of his neck, clearly uncomfortable with the praise. "It was, uh, Criminal Justice."

Sophie felt a triumphant grin spread across her face, "See? Are you trying to tell me that this wasn't your goal when you went for that degree?"

"Alright, alright, you got me. I really fucking want this job. But I'm still young to be considered for such a huge promotion. I don't want to get my hopes up."

Before Sophie could respond, they were called into an exam room. Butterflies took flight in her stomach. She was about to see her baby, about to hear its heartbeat for the very first time. She was equal parts thrilled and terrified.

CHAPTER SEVENTEEN

THE MOMENT the ultrasound image filled the screen and Rafe saw his baby, he was a goner. Nothing could have gotten him to tear his eyes away from that picture. The baby was so tiny, but the shape was there—little arms and fingers, legs and feet already formed. When the doctor allowed them to hear the heartbeat, and the sound filled the room, Rafe let out an audible gasp. That was his child on the screen. He was listening to *his child's* heartbeat.

He had to close his eyes to keep tears from falling. He was a father. For the first time in his life, he had a family. Sophie would never be able to understand the sheer magnitude of what she was giving him. He had never loved anything as much as he loved that kumquat-sized little being.

He felt a hand grasp his and looked down to see Sophie's hand in his own. He squeezed her hand tightly before returning his eyes to the screen. He wanted to ask if they could get a video and picture of the ultrasound, but he didn't trust his voice. Sophie threaded her fingers through his and asked the doctor to give them a moment alone.

"You okay over there?"

Rafe nodded, a small smile forming on his lips. He cleared his throat before responding.

"I'm incredible, Sophie." He turned to her, lightly planting a kiss on her forehead. "Thank you so much."

Sophie laughed, but he could see the unshed tears in her eyes as well. "Hey, it took two people to make that little girl."

Rafe groaned. "This again? You will give me a son, woman."

"Keep dreaming, big guy."

Rafe left the precinct that afternoon feeling as though he'd just nailed the most important interview of his career thus far. Everything had gone well; he'd answered the sergeant's questions thoroughly and confidently, never shying away from the tough inquiries. Though the sergeant wasn't able to give him a definitive answer right then and there, he'd told Rafe he'd done well.

Not wanting to share this moment with anyone else, he called Sophie the moment he got into his car. They hadn't spoken on the phone before—communicating primarily via text—but he wanted to hear her voice when he told her about the interview.

"Hey!" she answered enthusiastically. "How did the interview go?"

"Sophie, I fucking killed it."

"I knew you would. I'm really struggling not to say 'I told you so right now.' I won't say it, but I did."

Rafe laughed. "Yeah, you did. I think today has been the best day of my life. There is just one thing that could make it better."

"Oh? What's that?"

"Sophie, have dinner with me."

There was a pause at the other end of the phone. "Not like a date or anything, right? Just dinner?"

"Exactly like a date. Dinner, movies, mini golf—anything you want."

"Rafe, I'm not sure. I like our friendship as it is. I don't want to make anything awkward."

"Fuck awkward, Soph. It's just one date."

"Alright, how about a compromise? You come with me to Becky's birthday party tomorrow. It can be kind of like a trial run. If it goes well, I'll let you take me on a real date."

"Done."

Sophie laughed. "Oh, you're going to regret responding so quickly. Becky's birthday party is at a club downtown."

Rafe groaned. He hated clubs. He'd gone once in his early twenties and had only made it an hour before walking out. The pounding music and drunk idiots gave him a headache. But if this was the only shot Sophie was willing to give him, he'd take it.

"Alright, Sophie. I'm in, but if I do this, I want you to guarantee me at least five dates."

"Three."

"Four."

"I stand firm at three." She laughed.

"Fine. Just know that if you want to keep seeing me after

those three dates, you have to ask *me* out. I want romance, Soph."

"Well, aren't you confident? alright, I'll meet you at the club tomorrow night at ten."

"Bullshit, I'll be at your house at 9:30."

Sophie sighed and hung up on him. Rafe wore the biggest grin for the remainder of his drive home.

Rafe pulled into Sophie's driveway promptly at 9:25. He threw his car in park and ran his fingers through his hair. He'd actually bothered to style it a little, but was worried it made him look like a douche nozzle. He quickly got out of his car and made his way to the front door. If he thought about it too much, he'd spend another thirty minutes messing with his hair. He just wanted everything to be perfect.

He wasn't sure what he was expected to wear to a club, so he'd thrown on his nicest pair of dark-wash jeans and a black button-down. He despised how constricting the damn thing was, so the sleeves were rolled up to his elbows and the collar was open. He rang the doorbell, but only heard loud music and chaos in the house. Rafe tried knocking loudly, to no avail. After fifteen minutes of waiting, he tested the doorknob and found it unlocked. He walked inside and felt his eyes immediately widen.

There was shit everywhere. Clothes and shoes were

strewn across the living room, and there were shoes lined up on the normally immaculate coffee table.

"Sophie?" he called out tentatively. He recognized the blaring music and immediately rolled his eyes. *The Greatest Showman*, again. Rafe knew for a fact that Sophie and Kelsey watched the damn movie almost daily.

Receiving no response, he called out again, "Soph?"

An auburn head popped out of the hallway leading to the bedrooms. Kelsey waved at Rafe and grinned. "Take a seat, we're almost ready." She then proceeded to run past the doorway to the hall, allowing Rafe to catch a brief glimpse of way more skin than he needed to see from Sophie's best friend. Apparently the girls were still trying on clothes and had only gotten as far as underwear. Rafe sighed and took a seat on the couch.

As he'd guessed, *The Greatest Showman* was playing on the living room TV. Finding the remote under a stiletto on the table, he started the movie over. He needed to figure out what was so great about this damn thing. Since he apparently had some time to spare, he might as well get started now.

Forty-five minutes later, Rafe was hooked. He wasn't usually one for musicals, but this shit was *good*. It was only when he heard a throat clear that he saw Sophie and Kelsey standing in the doorway to the hall, watching him with bemused expressions. He paused the movie and took his time checking out Sophie.

She looked incredible in a fitted dress with slender straps. The dress was molded to her body, but long enough to remain respectable. As was fitting for a club, it was black and sparkly. She'd paired it with a pair of red fuck-me heels that had him practically drooling. Her long, blonde hair was pulled into a loose knot at the top of her head, a few strands escaping and curling down her neck and across her collarbone.

Rafe had never been a fan of too much makeup on the women he dated, preferring the natural look, but Sophie's makeup was tasteful and subtle with the exception of her cherry red lips. The lipstick she wore accentuated the bow shape of her gorgeous lips, giving him the most delicious vision of Sophie on her knees, performing acts he really shouldn't be thinking about now.

Rafe's personal favorite thing about Sophie's outfit though? The tiny baby bump he could make out through her dress. She was right—it was slight, and was probably just the result of water weight, but it reminded him that this woman was carrying his child. He stood up off the couch and walked over to Sophie, leaning over to kiss her cheek.

"You look incredible," he whispered in her ear, before planting another small kiss in the place her shoulder met her neck. He felt her shiver against his lips and stepped back. He was debating the likelihood of Sophie skipping this whole night to stay in bed with him when he heard Kelsey clear her throat.

"Hey, jackass. I look pretty fucking great too, thanks for noticing."

Rafe let out a chuckle. "You look fantastic, Kelsey. Are you riding with us to the club? I can go ahead and call an Uber."

Parking downtown was notoriously nightmarish, and he wanted to have a few beers while he was there. Driving with even one drink in his system wasn't something Rafe would ever do, and he didn't want Sophie to have to worry about driving.

Finally, at ten-thirty, the trio pulled up outside of the club. Rafe could hear the music pouring from the building and was already dreading this night. Maybe he would have a Jack on the rocks instead. Beer suddenly didn't seem like enough to get him through this. Sophie noticed him lingering near the car, clearly reluctant to enter the building. She walked over and grabbed his hand, linking their fingers and pulling them toward the bouncer.

"Come on, big guy. A little fun won't hurt you."

Rafe grumbled and followed her inside.

As he had expected, there were drunk fucking morons everywhere, gyrating and screaming, and sloshing drinks all over the already sticky floor. The temperature inside was stifling, making him wish he'd worn a T-shirt. He kept his grasp firm in Sophie's as she led them through the club to a roped-off section. When they were within sight of the area, an energetic, screaming redhead flew past the ropes and into Sophie's arms. Sophie released his hand to hug her back before she moved on to hug Kelsey.

"Fucking *finally*!" she screamed. "My party started an hour ago, you bitches!"

Sophie laughed, gesturing at herself. "Hey, looking this good takes some work. Becky, this is Rafe."

Becky turned her attention to Rafe, her eyes slowly skimming his body before lingering on his face. She stuck her hand out. "So you're the man behind that sexy voice. I swear, the first time Sophie played me that clip of your interview I came in my seat."

Rafe felt himself blush and he coughed, looking at Sophie. "Well, um, thank you?"

Sophie was practically doubled over laughing at his discomfort. "Wow, so you really were channeling Carlos during that interview, huh? The Rafe I met on that first day would have definitely made some lewd remark."

Rafe shrugged, but before he could respond, a hand clamped down on his shoulder.

"There you are, man! Could your invitation have been more vague? 'Sophie and I are going to a club downtown.' Do you know how many clubs there are downtown? This is the third one I've been in."

Rafe turned to his friend. "Carlos, that wasn't an invitation. You asked what I was doing and I told you."

Carlos shrugged. "Whatever you say. We both knew it wouldn't be a party without me." He kissed Sophie on the cheek and threw a head nod Kelsey's way.

"Hey Kels, looking fine as hell tonight."

Kelsey looked uncomfortable for a moment before responding. "Oh, hey Carlos. Thank you. Becky, where are the drinks?"

Becky grabbed Kelsey and Sophie by their hands and led them through the velvet rope to the table where she'd ordered bottle service. Rafe's eyes flicked back to Carlos. His friend was watching Kelsey walk away, looking slightly dejected. He shrugged it off quickly and turned to Rafe.

"Looks like they only have vodka and tequila up there. I'm gonna go grab us some whiskey from the bar."

Rafe nodded. "Thanks, man, that would be great."

A while later, Rafe had to admit he was having a pretty great time. Becky was hilarious, telling stories about her most horrific failed Tinder dates.

"There was this one guy who messaged me asking if I liked mustache rides." She laughed, tipping her head back to take another shot.

Sophie leaned forward. "Becky, didn't you go on a date with that guy?"

"Well, yeah." The redhead shrugged. "I fucking love mustache rides!"

The entire table burst out laughing. This girl was too much. She actually reminded him of Carlos in a lot of ways and he couldn't help but wonder if his friend would be better off pursuing her instead of Kelsey. Sophie's best friend had been practically ignoring Carlos all night, talking instead to the other girls in the group.

Carlos finished his drink and slammed it down on the table before standing. "Kelsey, come dance with me," he said, sticking his hand out to her.

Kelsey hesitated, looking around at her circle of friends before shaking her head. "I'm not in the mood to dance, Carlos."

"Oh come on..." He grinned. "I'm an excellent dancer. My mom tells me so all the time."

Kelsey smiled but shook her head. "I'm not sure it's really something that *friends* do," she replied, putting extra emphasis on the word *friends*.

Carlos dropped his hand, but before he could respond a pair of blondes walked up to the area they were seated in. One of them leaned across the rope, sticking her chest out, her obviously fake tits practically falling out of the tiny dress she was wearing.

"Excuse me," she said in a sickly sweet voice. "Are you two the 'Houston's Finest' cops that were featured in the newspaper?"

Rafe rolled his eyes and threw his arm around Sophie, hoping to make it clear he wasn't interested. But Carlos, having just been rejected in front of everyone, sauntered over to the pair.

"Why, yes, we are." He grinned. "I'm Carlos, and that over there is Rafe. He's a taken man, but I'm just here with *friends*. How about we go take some shots?"

The pair giggled, one of them resting her hand on Carlos's chest as she leaned forward to whisper in his ear. Rafe couldn't hear what she said, but Carlos's answering grin made the subject matter pretty clear.

"Sounds like a fun night. Count me in."

He unlatched the velvet rope and threw one arm around each girl's shoulder. Carlos turned back to look at Kelsey. "Don't wait up, friends."

As a whole, the group turned to look at Kelsey, who was staring at Carlos's retreating back as though willing him to turn around. Becky started to wrap Kelsey in a hug, but Kelsey shook her off, picking up the bottle of vodka on the table and taking a shot straight from its mouth.

"I think I'm going to go dance after all." She smiled at the group and walked out onto the dance floor.

Rafe, whose arm was still wrapped around Sophie, placed a hand on her thigh and leaned in. "What do you say we go dance too?"

He started drawing circles on her leg, each one creeping slowly upward. Sophie shivered in his arms and looked up at him. Her hair had fallen out of her messy bun almost completely and he ran one hand up the back of her neck. He pulled the hair tie gently from her blonde locks, watching them cascade down onto her shoulders.

Sophie's lips parted, her breath coming more heavily than before. Rafe stood up and pulled her to her feet, no longer waiting for a response. He led her to the dance floor and wrapped her in his arms as a song with a slow, thumping beat came through the speakers. Rafe fitted her body to his, wrapping one arm around her waist while the other roamed her curves. Sophie locked her hands behind Rafe's head, fitting one of his legs between hers as they grinded to the beat, completely lost in one another.

They danced until they were both sweaty, several songs passing, as they stood in the middle of the dance floor. Rafe leaned down and gently brushed his lips over hers as he pulled her hips into his, grinding his erection into her. Sophie moaned in his mouth, digging her fingers into his hair to deepen the kiss. He ran his tongue over the seam of her lips, requesting entry and when she opened for him, his desire broke free.

Their kiss turned brutal and passionate, tongues tangling, as Sophie continued to grind against Rafe's leg, her hands pulling softly on his hair. Rafe was rock hard and ready to take her right here on the dance floor, when he felt a hand on his shoulder. He growled and broke the kiss, turning to punch the shit out of whomever had dared to interrupt them.

Carlos held his hands up. "Whoa, man, sorry to interrupt your public fuck-fest, but have you seen Kelsey?"

Sophie looked around, and Rafe was pleased to see that her lips were swollen, her hair in disarray from his fingers. Unable to let go of her completely, Rafe kept his arm around Sophie's waist as he turned to scan the dance floor for Kelsey. When he finally spotted her auburn hair, he saw that she was dancing with some dickwad in a pink polo. The guy's hands were roaming her body freely as she grinded into him. He looked away quickly, trying to find something to distract Carlos, but when he looked at his friend, his eyes were already locked on the pair.

Carlos's features hardened, mouth falling into a straight line, his hands making fists at his sides. Rafe put a calming hand on Carlos's arm. "Hey, maybe she isn't interested, man. This shit isn't worth starting a fight over. Think of your badge."

Carlos shook off Rafe's hand, his eyes still fixated on Kelsey. He tensed as though preparing to storm over there, and then deflated. Carlos looked down at the ground, shaking his head. "Yeah, I'm gonna get out of here."

Sophie spoke up at Rafe's side. "Wait, where are those two badge bunnies you were with? They looked like they wanted to fuck your brains out in the club bathroom."

Carlos smiled. "Not really my style, shortcake. We took a few shots, and they were drunk as hell so I put them in a cab."

"Hey man, we'll leave with you. I can already feel the headache coming on."

Carlos waved them off. "Nah, you two have fun. I'll see you at work tomorrow."

CHAPTER EIGHTEEN

SOPHIE WOKE up the next morning with the biggest smile on her face. Kelsey-and-Carlos drama aside, she'd had an amazing night with Rafe. He'd been so wonderful with her friends, laughing at all of the right times, jumping in with fun stories from his time on the force, and just generally being charming. He'd remained by her side throughout the whole night, making her feel like the most beautiful woman in the room. His eyes had never strayed, despite the number of scantily clad women around.

When she had originally made the deal with him—three dates if last night went well—she hadn't expected to feel this way. She'd thought he would return to being the cocky, arrogant player he'd been when she first met him. Apparently though, Rafe really had been channeling Carlos the day of their first interview. Sure, he'd been an insufferable flirt with her when they first met, but he hadn't flirted with any other women in front of her. In fact, she hadn't even seen him glance another woman's way.

Sophie placed a hand on her stomach, trying to remind

herself that a few weeks of good behavior on his part didn't make him any less of a player. Maybe the guy was just a good actor. Her exes had seemed sweet enough when she'd started dating them too. Even though they'd been charming at first, Shane and Charlie had checked out women in front of her, even on their first dates. She'd always brushed it off as a "guy thing," but Rafe seemed different.

The whole thing was confusing the hell out of her. She knew that she'd promised him three dates, and she was going to follow through. After the third date though, they needed to remain friends. It was the only way that they could be successful co-parents. She wouldn't let this get out of hand. Losing his support would make her life ten times harder. At least she could allow herself a little bit of fun for three dates. Surely, that couldn't hurt anything.

Sophie rolled over when she heard her phone chime from her bedside table. Another smile broke over her face. The only person who ever texted her first thing in the morning was Rafe. She couldn't wait to see what he had to say after their night together.

Rafe: Last night was fun.

Sophie: It wasn't so bad. I guess you're an alright dancer.

Rafe: Alright? I'm a fucking fantastic dancer. One more song and I would have had you coming on that dance floor.

Desire hit Sophie hard, making her body flush and setting her nerve endings on fire. That dance had been incredible, and the kiss had been quite possibly the best of her life. Rafe's hands around her waist, her hands tugging on his hair, his erection grinding into her hip while she rubbed herself against his strong thigh. He wasn't wrong; she'd been one song away from an orgasm.

> **Sophie:** I think you overestimate your skill, big guy.
>
> **Rafe:** Well, you've got the big part right. This conversation is only making it bigger...
>
> **Rafe:** And I call bullshit. I'm willing to bet you're as turned on as I am right now.
>
> **Sophie:** Sounds like you need a cold shower.
>
> **Rafe:** Well, I am about to hop in the shower. I just got back from the gym and I now have a problem I need to take care of...

Sophie clenched her thighs together in an attempt to alleviate some of the pressure building between them. Thoughts of Rafe naked, drenched in sweat from his morning workout, filtered through her head. She was just contemplating grabbing her vibrator from her nightstand, when her phone went off in her hand again.

> **Rafe:** No response? Are your hands too busy to text, Sophie?
>
> **Sophie:** One of them might be...

Rafe: Jesus, Soph, what are you doing to me?

Sophie: I'm personally more interested in what you're doing to yourself.

Rafe: Currently, I'm picturing you on your knees in front of me, your mouth replacing my hand on my cock.

Rafe: My hand is on the back of your head, guiding your rhythm, and your hand is between your thighs, rubbing your clit in circles.

Shit, he's good at this. Sophie almost reached for her vibrator but decided to instead use her fingers, sticking to the image Rafe was creating.

Sophie: Fast circles or slow circles, Rafe?

Rafe: Shit, Sophie. Please tell me you're actually touching yourself.

Sophie: Are you?

Rafe: Fuck yes I am, are you crazy?

Sophie: So what happens next, Rafe?

Rafe: To start, your fingers are rubbing your clit in slow circles, to match the pace of your mouth on me.

Rafe: And then I start to move my hips, needing more. Your hand speeds up too.

Sophie: Keep going.

Rafe: Just when you're about to come, I pull you to your feet and get down on my knees to return the favor, sucking your clit into my mouth, pushing two fingers into you.

As she read his texts, Sophie continued to rub her clit with her thumb, following his instructions and pushing two fingers inside.

Sophie: Rafe, I'm close.

Rafe: No ma'am, not yet. We come together, Sophie. I lift you off of your feet, set you on the counter, and push into you. I move my thumb to your clit, rubbing gently as I fuck you on the counter.

Sophie: If you want me to finish with you, you need to hurry up. I'm already close.

Rafe: Shit, Sophie. I'm close. Come with me.

Sophie was close too, her fingers and thumb increasing in speed until she shattered. She bit her lip to contain the moan building in her throat as her orgasm washed over her.

Rafe: Fuuuuuuck that was good. I wish you were here. I just came all over my damn sink.

Sophie laughed, finding the thought of Rafe having to clean his sink hilarious for some reason. That had been the best orgasm she'd had since...well, the supply closet.

Sophie: I should probably get out of bed and take a shower now.

Rafe: Ha. Me too, I actually have to work today.

Before Sophie could respond, she heard a loud pounding coming from the front of the house. As the sound grew more persistent, she pulled on a pair of shorts and a tank top, before wrapping her robe around her body. The racket was coming from the front door, and as she went to answer it, Kelsey came out of her room down the hall.

Sophie opened the door to Kelsey's livid ex-husband, Kyle. He appeared to have been in mid-knock, his fist still raised in the air.

Kelsey came up behind Sophie. "Kyle, what the hell are you doing here?"

Pushing his way past the two women, Kyle strode into the living room before turning to face them. "Where the fuck is my son, Kelsey? It's supposed to be my goddamn weekend with him."

Sophie unlocked her phone, pulling up Rafe's contact and holding her thumb over the call button. Kyle wasn't a violent man, but the divorce seemed to have changed him. Before this morning, Sophie had never heard him raise his voice at Kelsey.

Kelsey stood her ground. "I told you yesterday that I needed you to take James last night, Kyle. You didn't answer a single fucking phone call or text, so I took him to my parent's house."

"Sorry I don't want to watch my son so that you can whore yourself around tow—"

Sophie had had enough. "You're done, Kyle. Get the fuck out of my house."

Kyle laughed. "What the hell are you gonna do, Sophie? You're all of five feet. You can't force me to do shit."

"Oh really? I happen to have an HPD officer on goddamn speed dial. Get out of my house before he comes to remove you."

Apparently not wanting to deal with the police, Kyle walked toward the front door. "Kelsey, I'll be back at noon to pick up my son. He better fucking be here."

Kyle slammed the door as he left, and Sophie quickly hurried to lock it behind him. When she returned to the living room, she found Kelsey curled up on the couch, her head in her hands. Sophie wrapped her arms around her best friend, offering what comfort she could.

"Kels, how long has it been like this? You never told me it was that bad."

Kelsey looked up, tears streaming down her face. "He's been like this since I filed for divorce. He's so angry with me, all the time. But he's still a fantastic father to James, so I just don't know what to do."

Sophie thought about the night before and how much worse things would've been had Carlos been at the house this morning. Suddenly, her friend's behavior toward him made sense.

"So that's why you're pushing Carlos away—you don't

want to drag him into this."

Kelsey sniffed and nodded. "My life is a fucking shitshow. I'm not ready, and he deserves better. Maybe one of those badge bunnies from last night has what he's looking for."

"Hey, you're the fucking best. Plus, Carlos didn't go home with either of those women last night. He put them in a cab and came back inside looking for you."

Kelsey nodded again. "It doesn't change anything, Soph. I'm not in the right state of mind to date. I need to figure out what the hell to do with Kyle."

"Let me ask Rafe. Maybe we can look into filing a restraining order?"

"No, I can't do that to Kyle. Like I said, he's great with James; it's me he's mad at. I need to think of another way to handle this."

Kelsey got up off of the couch and wiped the tears from her eyes. "I'm going to go take a shower and pick up James. Thank you, Soph. I don't know what I'd do without you."

One steaming hot shower and delicious cup of herbal tea later, Sophie found herself on the couch staring at her phone. She pulled her feet up onto the couch and under her, contemplating the call she was about to make. She was eleven weeks pregnant and still hadn't told her father. She and her dad had a tricky relationship; in her early twenties, Sophie had been a bit of a handful. She'd flitted from job to job and partied way too much with her friends. Though she'd made it through college, she hadn't gotten the best GPA and had gotten a degree she didn't really care much for. Those years had put a strain on her relationship with her dad, who had higher expectations of her and was, frankly, a little bit of a hardass. Her early twenties were a distant memory, but she was still struggling to build a strong relationship with her only parent. Her mother had left her when she was still a child, and it had always been her and her dad.

She was honestly dreading telling him about the baby. Sophie could practically hear his judgment and disappointment in her head. Before she could give herself a chance to back out, she hit the call button. The phone rang twice before her father's voice came through the phone.

"Jim Klein," he answered, curtly. He always answered the phone the exact same way, even when he knew it was Sophie calling.

"Hey Dad," Sophie said meekly, already losing her courage. Few people could make Sophie nervous, and her father was certainly one of them.

"Hey sweet pea! Haven't heard from you in weeks! What's new?"

"Well, um, that's actually what I called to speak to you about." She tried to force as much cheer into her voice as possible. "I have news!"

"Okay," he replied cautiously. Her dad always knew when she was scared to tell him something.

"Impregnant," she blurted.

"Soph, I didn't catch that." He chuckled. "Try telling me again at the speed of a normal human, not an auctioneer."

Sophie took a deep breath and repeated herself. "I'm pregnant."

"Oh, wow! I didn't even know you were seeing anyone, sweet pea. Did you just find out? Who is this guy? Are you engaged too?"

"Well I'm not seeing him...the father, that is. His name is Rafe and it was a, um. I mean, we aren't dating. But that's okay! I'm about eleven weeks along and all is healthy."

"What do you mean you're not dating him?"

"He's just a friend?" Sophie asked, her tone implying a question, not a statement.

"Hmm."

"That's okay though, Dad! He's a good guy, a police officer actually. Plus, he's been here every step of the way. Things are fine, I promise."

"Hmm," he repeated, his inflection not changing at all.

"You're going to be a grandfather! Isn't that exciting?"

Her father's voice immediately softened. "Well, of course, that's exciting. I can't wait to meet my grandchild. But are you sure you're okay? Maybe you should move home and let me help you."

Sophie scoffed, "Dad, we would drive each other crazy within a week. How about I come visit you sometime this month? I'll drive up and stay, and you can see the ultrasound."

"You mean *you'd* drive *me* crazy. I'm the sane one in this family."

"Where do you think I get my crazy from? So, I'll see you next weekend?"

"Sounds good, sweet pea. Don't forget that ultrasound."

"I won't, Dad. Love you."

"Love you too, kid."

CHAPTER NINETEEN

Rafe: You owe me 3 dates, woman.

Sophie: Ummm wrong number?

Rafe: Ha ha, very funny. You should just go ahead and save me as "Best Sex I've Ever Had."

Sophie: You're currently saved under "Double Bagger."

Rafe: You wound me, Sophie. According to the women of Houston, I'm fine as helllll.

Sophie: Did you just hear my eye roll? I eye-rolled so hard that I'm sure people in Canada heard it.

Rafe: Wait...that's not really my name in your phone, right?

Incoming photo from Sophie

Rafe: SOPH! My fragile ego can't handle these insults! Change it right now.

Sophie: Alright, changed it.

Rafe: What did you change it to??

Sophie: Pencil Dick

Rafe: WHOA! Now you're insulting Little Rafe? Don't make me send a dick pic as proof.

Sophie: Not changing it.

Rafe: I'll do it, Sophie. Don't test me.

Rafe: Hold on, making Carlos pull the patrol car over so I can run into this Whataburger.

Sophie: A Whataburger dick pic...really classy, Rafe.

Rafe: MY DIGNITY IS AT STAKE HERE, SOPHIE.

Sophie: What reason are you giving Carlos for this sudden pit stop?

Rafe: I told him I had to pee.

Sophie: You know, you really should be honest with your partner.

Rafe: YOU TEXTED HIM?

Rafe: WHY DO YOU EVEN HAVE HIS NUMBER?

Rafe: I WILL NEVER LIVE THIS DOWN. HE'S CALLING ME OFFICER PENCIL DICK, SOPHIE.

Sophie: Alright, calm down, Mister Shouty Pants. I got his number from Kelsey.

Sophie: Rafe?

Sophie: Hello?

Sophie: Are you pouting?

Rafe: I'm brooding. Men fucking brood, Sophie. I'm a man. A handsome, well endowed MAN dammit.

Sophie: Okay, okay. I changed your name in my phone.

Incoming photo from Sophie

Rafe: Officer Pencil Dick? Really? REALLY?

Rafe: That's it, going into the Whataburger bathroom now.

Incoming photo from Rafe

Sophie: Rafe, why is there a dick on my phone screen right now?

Rafe: You made me do it.

Sophie: Okay, I really want to know where you got the measuring tape.

Rafe: Don't worry about it.

Sophie: Please tell me you didn't buy it for this picture.

Rafe: IT NEEDED TO BE DONE, SOPHIE. Now change my fucking name.

Sophie: Okay, this is the last time I'm changing it. You're saved as Baby Daddy now.

Rafe: That's right, I am your baby daddy. Don't you forget it.

Sophie: Rolling my eyes again, Rafe.

Rafe: So about this date. I'll pick you up tomorrow night at 6.

Sophie: I have plans to wash my hair.

Rafe: Oh, shower date? I'll help.

Sophie: You are insufferable. Fine, see you at 6.

Rafe: Dress sexy, Baby Momma.

THOUGH SOPHIE WOULD NEVER ADMIT it to Rafe, she was looking forward to their date tonight. She'd even gone shopping for a dress to wear. Her baby bump had come in seemingly overnight and she felt bloated in everything she currently owned. She looked in the mirror and ran her hands down the dress she chose. It was a black peplum dress and hugged her curves while managing to hide her baby bump. She'd paired it with her favorite red pumps, a pearl necklace, and understated pearl studs. Kelsey had done her makeup: a very light and natural cat eye with red lipstick.

For the first time in weeks, Sophie actually felt attractive. When she heard a knock at the door, she gave herself one final lookover in the mirror before heading out into the living room. Kelsey had let Rafe in, and he was holding James. He was tugging on Rafe's ear while babbling away. Apparently James wanted Rafe to know that he was successfully pooping in the potty.

Rafe was laughing and congratulating the little guy, not even a little bothered by the ear pulling and incessant chatter. For most people, James was a little too much. He was a pretty hyperactive three-year-old and was surprisingly loquacious for his age.

While he was distracted, Sophie took a moment to drink Rafe in. He was wearing gray slacks and a green button-down, the pants hugging him in all of the right places. She watched his muscles flex when he shifted James from one side of his body to the other and actually felt saliva pool in her mouth. He was too handsome; it was honestly unfair. She hoped their child got his genes. Sophie could already picture it: a little girl with Rafe's blonde hair and blue eyes, a mischievous little smile pulling at her lips. She smiled and rubbed a hand over her small bump. With every day that passed, she grew more attached to her baby, more sure of her choice.

Seeing Rafe with James warmed her heart. He was going to be such an incredible father: attentive, loving, and playful. She could feel herself softening toward him and knew she needed to tread carefully. Sophie had hated him when they'd first met, but as Rafe had gotten to know her, he'd opened up to her more. Sure, he was still a cocky asshole from time to time, but he also made her laugh, brought her pie when she was craving it, and made her feel sexy in a time when her body wasn't quite feeling like her own. She knew with a startling certainty that she could fall for him, and that terrified her. She hated to give anyone that kind of power over her, but she didn't know how to stop her growing emotions.

Rafe looked up and met Sophie's eyes, a small smile forming on his lips. He gave James a little squeeze before setting him down and walking toward Sophie slowly. The toddler ran into the living room, Kelsey throwing Sophie a wink before following her son. Rafe grabbed Sophie's hand, turning it over to place a light kiss on the inside of her wrist, just over her pulse point.

"You look stunning, Sophie," he said in a soft voice. His eyes ran over her slowly, heat blooming everywhere they touched. When his eyes reached hers again, she saw lust in them. Suddenly, her day of shopping and primping all seemed worth it.

Realizing she hadn't spoken since he walked in, Sophie put up her hand for an awkward little wave. "Hi."

Rafe laughed and took her hand, twining their fingers together and pulling her out the door. Sophie didn't have a shy bone in her body, but she was suddenly nervous and couldn't seem to find her voice. Something about the tender look he'd given her, the way he'd kissed her pulse before reverently taking her in had gotten to her. She wasn't sure how to act around this sweeter, softer version of Rafe.

He opened the car door for her before moving to his side of the vehicle. Sophie still hadn't found her voice when he got in the car and pulled out of her driveway. Talking suddenly seemed so daunting, and she didn't want to mess this up. History had proven that Sophie and Rafe could easily start a fight, and Sophie was reluctant to ruin the calm of their night. Instead of talking, she picked at the nail polish on her fingers, fidgeting in her seat.

"Alright, Sophie. What the hell is going on? You're never this quiet and it's freaking me out."

Sophie laughed, "Don't make fun of me, okay?" She heaved a heavy sigh and spoke quickly, her words slurring together. "Imnervous."

Rafe laughed, his head falling back to meet the headrest as the sound of his joyful outburst filled the car. Sophie reached over and hit him with her clutch. "Asshole!"

He held up his hand to defend himself. "I'm sorry, I'm sorry. Just the idea of you being nervous is so absurd to me. You're one of the most confident women I've ever met. It's one of your sexier qualities."

Sophie snorted, "You're such a dick sometimes."

"It's charming, isn't it?" he joked, throwing a wink her way. "Alright, let's find a way to make you less nervous. Have you ever played the question game?"

Sophie shook her head.

"Alright, so we take turns asking questions. They can be about anything, and we have to agree to answer with complete honesty, okay?"

"You know I'm a reporter, right? This is a dangerous game you're playing, Officer Pencil Dick."

Rafe scowled. "I thought we agreed to never discuss that again. Do I need to send you another picture?"

Sophie laughed. "Alright, I'll drop it. You ask first, pretty boy."

"Not liking the nicknames tonight, Soph. But okay, I'll go first. What color thong are you wearing?"

Her eyes rolled, seemingly of their own volition, and she decided to torture him with a little white lie. "Actually, I'm not wearing any underwear," she replied smugly.

Rafe made a choked sound, his grip tightening on the steering wheel. "You fight dirty, Sophie Klein."

Sophie shrugged. "You told me to be honest." She knew it was her turn and was already struggling to come up with a question. She decided to start out easy. "What's your favorite color?"

Rafe glanced over, his eyes moving quickly down her body before landing on her shoes. A small smile tipped up the corner of his mouth. "Right now, I'm really loving red." His gaze flicked back up to hers. "And green. I find myself liking the color green more and more."

Sophie smiled and blushed, his compliment washing over her. Before she could respond, he asked his next question. They continued asking back and forth for the duration of their car ride. She learned that Rafe listened primarily to classic rock and was allergic to shellfish. She told him that she'd always wanted to work for a publisher in New York and that she hated bacon. He'd almost kicked her out of his car after hearing the last admission.

By the time they pulled up to the restaurant, Sophie's nervousness had abated. The question game had done exactly what Rafe had wanted—it had gotten her out of her own head. Before she could open the car door, Rafe came around and opened it for her, offering his hand.

The restaurant he had chosen was an Italian place she'd seen plenty of times on her way home and had always wanted to try. They were seated quickly at a quiet two-top in the corner of the room. The lights were dimmed, creating a private ambiance. There was a small tea-light candle on the table, casting a soft, flickering light that added to the romantic atmosphere. Rafe pulled out her chair before seating himself, and she smiled at the sweet gesture.

Sophie was looking over the menu, trying to decide what she wanted, when their server approached. She was stunning, with long, blonde hair loosely curled and pinned away from her face. She wore a standard uniform for a waitress: black pants, black button-down shirt, and black apron, but on her it looked incredible. Oh, and she was looking at Rafe like she wanted to eat him up.

"Good evening," she said, eyes never leaving Rafe. "My name is Shelby and I'll be taking care of you this evening. What can I get you to drink?" Shelby offered Rafe a dazzling smile, not once looking at Sophie.

Rafe, for his part, seemed to be completely oblivious to the attention. "I'll take a glass of water please. What about you, Soph?" As he asked, he reached across the table, placing his hand over hers and rubbing lightly with his thumb.

The gesture did not go unnoticed by their server, and her eyes finally met Sophie's, narrowing. Sophie shifted uncomfortably and pulled her hand out from under Rafe's. She'd experienced this before with her exes. Charlie, for his part, had always assured Sophie that he only wanted to be with her, but she could always tell that he secretly enjoyed the attention. Feeling tense and uncomfortable again, Sophie quickly ordered her water and returned her gaze to the menu in front of her. She should have known this would happen. Dating Rafe was a terrible idea.

She knew she was being at least a little irrational. It wasn't Rafe's fault he was "Houston's Hot Cop," but when she'd brushed things like this off in the past, she had been wrong to. Charlie had cheated on her, and she'd trusted him. She guessed a guy could only get hit on by so many attractive women before succumbing.

She was pulled from her introspection by Rafe himself. "Hey," he said softly. "Where did you go?"

He offered Sophie a warm smile and put his hand on hers again. She shook her head and smiled in return. If she was only going to let herself have a date with Rafe, she might as well enjoy it. She could ignore Shelby for now.

"Yeah, just trying to figure out what the hell to order. This menu is all in Italian, you know."

Rafe laughed. "The descriptions of the menu items are underneath in English."

Sophie looked down at her menu and found that he was right. She smiled sheepishly and picked up her menu to hide her blush. "Know it all," she murmured.

Rafe laughed again and pulled her menu down with his finger. "I've seen that menu plenty of times. I'd prefer to look at your face, Soph."

Before she could reply, our horny-for-Rafe waitress returned, batting her eyelashes at him as she approached. She placed Sophie's drink down with no care, some of the water sloshing over the side of the glass. Shelby put down Rafe's glass much more gently, leaning down and practically shoving her ample chest in his face.

Rafe didn't so much as glance at the cleavage that was practically under his nose and continued to look at Sophie, his hand still on hers. "Do you know what you want to order, *babe*?" He put extra emphasis on the endearment, having finally picked up on what Shelby was laying down.

Sophie raised her eyebrows, trying to contain her smile. "Why don't you order for me, *sugar bear*."

Rafe laughed loudly, his entire face lighting up with glee. He quickly placed their order, his lips caressing the syllables to form words she would have butchered. Damn, he was sexy when he spoke a foreign language.

Shelby, not one to be deterred or ignored, leaned forward once more. "I'll get this order placed for you, but if you need *anything* at all, please don't hesitate to ask." As she spoke, she slid a piece of receipt paper across the table at Rafe. Was this hussy slipping Rafe her number *in front of his date?* Sophie looked to Rafe, trying to judge his reaction, and saw his jaw clench. Oh, he was *pissed*.

He slowly picked the piece of paper up off of the table and, without glancing at it, crumpled it in his fist. "I'm sorry," he gritted out, jaw still clenching. "Are you hitting on me in front of my fucking date?"

Shelby stuttered out her response, "Well I just recognized you from Instagram. You're the hot cop. I thought you might want to have a little bit of fun after you take *her* home."

Rafe was clearly fighting for control, his hand now forming a fist on the table. Sophie reached out and covered his fist with her own hand. "Rafe, it's fine. We can go. Just take me home, okay?"

He looked up and met her eyes, his blue eyes burning. They softened when they met hers, and he took a deep breath. "Please go get your manager. I think your boss should know how you're treating *the mother of my child*."

At this, Shelby straightened. She stuttered out an apology before leaving in search of her manager. Sophie was honestly mortified and wanted nothing more than to go home. Before she could once again ask Rafe if they could leave, he picked up his chair and moved it to her side of the table. The small table was only meant to seat one person on each side, so it was a tight fit. Rafe reached up and brushed her hair off of her neck, squeezing to soothe her tense muscles. He leaned in and planted a kiss on her jaw before nibbling his way up to her ear.

"Sophie, I'm so sorry. I've been coming here for years and that has never happened before."

She couldn't think with him this close, his hand still

working her neck, his breath hot in her ear. She felt a shiver work its way through her body. She shrugged her shoulders and immediately felt his other hand on her cheek.

"Soph, look at me," he demanded quietly.

She looked up and met his gaze, his hand still gently cupping her cheek. His face was serious, but his eyes were warm on hers, the blue so deep it threatened to pull her in. He used the hand that had been rubbing her neck to gently tuck a piece of errant hair behind her ear.

"I'm here with you, only you. If tonight goes well, I plan to go home with you too. And tomorrow? I'll be thinking of you, not her. Just you."

He planted a tender kiss on her lips and she closed her eyes, sinking into it. She ran her tongue along the seam of his lips, looking to deepen the kiss. Instead of opening for her, Rafe offered her another gentle peck before pulling back.

"Trying to start a scene, Sophie?" He leaned in to whisper in her ear, "I've wanted to fuck you since I picked you up tonight. Keep kissing me like that and we won't make it to your house. Do you want me to get arrested for indecent exposure?"

Heat rushed through Sophie's body, her nipples tightening. His words brought to mind images of their brief encounter in the bar supply closet.

He grabbed her hand and brought it to his lap where he was hot and hard for her. His lips were still by her ear, his breath caressing her neck as he growled in her ear. "You do this to me, Sophie. Only you. When you walk into a room, I pop a boner like a fucking teenager. It's damn inconvenient in polyester pants, let me tell you."

She rubbed her hand over his erection and he groaned, low and husky, before he pulled her hand away, lacing his fingers through hers and placing their now joined hands on the table. Before he could say anything else the manager of the restaurant came to the table, apologizing profusely. She assured them that Shelby had been relieved of her position and offered to wait on them herself. The rest of their dinner went smoothly, and Rafe remained on her side of the table. Sophie was amused to learn that he was a food thief, sneaking bites from her plate when he thought she wasn't looking.

When the manager offered them dessert, Rafe looked at Sophie hotly, his eyes running down her body. He politely informed her that they had dessert waiting for them at home and asked for the bill. They left the restaurant hand in hand, and Rafe once again opened her car door for her. Once in the car, Sophie pulled her phone out of her purse. She hadn't looked at it throughout dinner and wanted to make sure that Kelsey was doing alright. She and Kyle had fought again today; he wasn't making their divorce easy at all. She didn't have any messages or calls from Kelsey, but she laughed at the message she saw from her dad.

It was a picture of him holding a swaddled watermelon proudly. He'd been practicing swaddling and diaper changing since she'd told him about the baby. After he'd gotten over the initial shock, he had been thrilled at the prospect of being a grandfather. Her dad had already bought a crib and high chair for his house. He said that he wanted grandchild time at least once per month and needed to be fully equipped.

"What's so funny?" Rafe asked from the driver's seat, a small smile pulling at the corner of his mouth.

"Oh, my dad is practicing diaper changing and swaddling on a watermelon apparently," she laughed. "I forgot to ask you, what did your parents say when you told them about the baby? Are they excited to be grandparents?"

Rafe's grip tightened on the steering wheel and he was silent for a moment before sighing. "I don't have parents. I was a foster child."

Sophie immediately reached across the car, wrapping his free hand around hers. "I'm so sorry, Rafe. I had no idea."

He shrugged and squeezed her hand. "It isn't something I like to talk about, but it doesn't matter anymore. You're giving me all of the family I'll ever need, Sophie."

Her breath caught in her chest. She'd known that he was excited about their baby, that it had meant something to him, but she never would've guessed how special this was for Rafe. Warmth washed over her as she thought about Rafe as a father. Before she could ask more about his family, he pulled the car into Sophie's driveway.

Suddenly nervous all over again, Sophie unbuckled her seatbelt and got out of the car before he could open her door. She knew what he wanted, and she absolutely wanted it too, but she wasn't exactly feeling sexy these days. The dress hid her protruding belly, but he would see it if they were naked together. Butterflies took flight in her stomach, making her almost nauseous as she approached her front door. She placed her key in the lock and turned to look at Rafe. He was standing closer than she expected, and her breath caught at the softness in his eyes.

He cupped her cheek gently and pulled her in for a kiss. His lips caressed hers softly before he deepened the kiss, his hand gliding down her side as his tongue stroked hers. She reached up and wrapped her fist around the fabric of his shirt, pulling his body into hers as she moved closer to the front door. When her back hit the door, he placed his hands on her waist, the kiss turning rougher. He ground his hips into her, his erection resting against her stomach. She was on the verge of jumping up and wrapping her legs around his waist when he pulled back with a groan.

"Shit, Sophie. Are you sure? I know what I said at the restaurant, but if you want to wait, we can wait. I'll go home right now if you want me to. Hell, I'll even hold you while we watch some stupid chick flick. You set the pace here."

As he spoke, his hands moved from her waist to her belly, touching the small bump there with reverence. All of her fears fled her mind as she looked into his face. He looked so earnest, and she'd felt how excited he was, how badly he wanted her. Yet he was willing to leave if it was what she wanted. Sophie thought about sending him home—they really should take things slow. But she didn't want slow; she wanted him. Without another word, she unlocked her front door and pulled Rafe through it.

CHAPTER TWENTY

THIS HADN'T BEEN Rafe's plan; he'd wanted to take Sophie to dinner, get to know her better, and then bring her home. He wouldn't lie and say he hadn't planned to kiss her good night and cop a feel, but he'd thought he would be going home alone, maybe spending a little quality time with his dick and hand. Now, with Sophie's soft hand in his, her mouthwatering ass leading him through the dark and quiet house, he knew he couldn't turn back for anything.

Fuck, I should go home.

His eyes dropped from her ass to the fuck-me heels she'd worn for him, and his dick twitched in his pants. He'd been hard since he'd placed her hand on his cock in the restaurant. The way he reacted to this woman was unnatural. He could lie to himself and pretend it was just the thrill of knowing that she was carrying his child, but deep down Rafe knew that it was Sophie. She fired him up like nobody else. Just standing in a room with her got him hot.

When he'd first seen her tonight in that tight black dress, her long, blonde hair flowing around her shoulders, he'd been tempted to say fuck the date and pull her back to her bedroom. He couldn't even count the number of times he'd come at home alone in his bed, her name a breath on his lips, as he recalled their night at the bar. It had been, without a doubt, the hottest sex of his life. He'd always been a fan of hard and rough sex, always making sure his partners got off before he did. Now, with Sophie, he had the sudden urge to savor her. Rafe wanted to take his time, learn all of the dips and curves of her delectable body.

Sophie pulled Rafe into her bedroom and closed the door. He sucked in a breath, recalling the last time he'd been in this room. He'd found out he was going to be a father here. His life had been changed irrevocably on the hardwood floor by Sophie's bed. He took in the details of the room—the white metal frame of her bed, the plum and gray bedding, and the small bookshelf pushed against the wall. The bookshelf was full, with books stacked on top. Sophie clearly needed another shelf.

He took a steadying breath as he returned his gaze to hers. Sophie's lips were swollen from his kiss, her eyes half lidded with lust. Using the hand he still held, he pulled her to him, her lush breasts meeting his chest as he wrapped an arm around her waist. Rafe leaned down to nuzzle her neck, planting small kisses as he worked his way up to her ear. Sophie's breath hitched and she let out a low, breathy moan.

"Are you sure, Sophie? If we start this, it won't end until I'm so deep inside you that you'll be feeling me for days. I want you so fucking badly I can't even think straight. This is your last chance to decide you want to take this slow."

"Rafe," Sophie moaned. "Why the fuck are you still talking? You could be inside me by now."

At that, Rafe snapped, crashing his mouth over hers. The

kiss he gave her wasn't the slow exploration he'd planned. He kissed Sophie with all of the built-up passion he had in him. His hands worked their way into her long hair, wrapping it around his fists as he tilted her head back, giving him more access. Sophie, never one to back down, gave as good as she got, twining her tongue with his and sucking his lower lip between hers to give it a teasing nip.

Rafe backed Sophie toward the bed, his lips never leaving hers. When the backs of her knees hit the mattress, he lifted her by her ass, breaking their kiss to toss her lightly onto the bed. He unbuttoned his shirt as quickly as possible, dropping it in a careless heap on the floor. He kicked off his shoes and socks before removing his boxers and dress pants. Sophie lay in the middle of the bed, her hair spread out under her, and her eyes on Rafe as he stripped for her. He ran his eyes down her body, taking in her perfect breasts, small waist, and full, rounded hips. Though she was short, her lean legs seemed to go on for miles. He reached down and took his throbbing cock in his hand, pumping himself once, his mouth watering as he thought of all of the things he wanted to do to Sophie's delectable body.

She began to sit up, reaching for the zipper on the back of her dress, her pretty green eyes never leaving his dick. She licked her lips as she watched him slowly stroke himself. Rafe released his dick and leaned over her on the bed, placing a hand on each side of her hips.

"Get your hands away from that zipper, Sophie. I'll be undressing you tonight." He stood back up and gently pushed her upper body back to the bed. "Hands above your head," he commanded. Heat flared in Sophie's eyes as she followed his orders, her back arching as she placed her hands above her head on the bed. Rafe reached for the bottom of her dress and she raised her hips slightly as he pushed it up, giving him a glimpse of the red lace thong she wore.

"Oh you lying minx," he breathed, smirking at Sophie. "No fucking underwear, huh? You're such a goddamn tease."

Seeing her splayed out for him like this, he knew he wouldn't last long inside of her. He needed to make her come at least once before he took her. Rafe hooked his arms under each of her legs and spread them, pulling her toward the edge of the bed as he got on his knees. He left her heels on and put one leg over each of his shoulders.

Rafe planted teasing kisses on the inside of her thighs, slowly working his way up. Sophie groaned through gritted teeth, "Rafe, stop fucking teasing me."

He laughed and ran his tongue up her slit through her underwear, soaking the material. "Is this where you want me, Sophie? You want my tongue here? My fingers? My cock?" Before she had a chance to respond, Rafe pushed aside her panties and ran his tongue over her clit.

"Fuck, you're so goddamn wet for me right now," he groaned.

Sophie let out a long moan as he returned to his ministrations. He feasted on her like a man starved, sucking her clit into his mouth as he filled her with his finger. Rafe licked, sucked, and fingered her until her legs began to clench around his head, her hand finding his hair and pulling. Knowing she was close to an orgasm, he slowed down and looked up at her. Her greedy green gaze drank him in as he licked her, and he stopped, pulling his finger out of her completely.

"Hands above your head, Sophie."

She removed her hand from his hair and returned it to its place. The moment her hand hit the bed, Rafe swiped his tongue through her slit, returning his focus to her clit as he thrust two fingers into her. She let out a long moan when he curled his fingers, searching for her sweet spot. He sucked her clit into his mouth and she screamed, her taste flooding his mouth as she came. He fingered her slowly through her orgasm, her eyes closed as her head thrashed on the bed.

When she'd come down, Rafe stood and pushed her dress the rest of the way up her body, revealing the sexiest red lace bra he'd ever seen. He drank her in greedily, slowly pushing one bra strap down her arm before freeing her breast from the cup of her bra. He sucked her nipple into his mouth and felt a shudder run through her body. While he sucked and nipped her right breast, his hand freed the left, pinching her nipple lightly. He moved his mouth to her left breast and his hands circled her to undo the bra clasp. Tossing her bra to the ground, he kissed his way down her body, returning to the lace thong—the only piece of clothing that still remained.

"Do you have any particular attachment to this?" Rafe asked, fingering the strap of her underwear.

Sophie shook her head and Rafe wasted no time, ripping it off of her and tossing away the scraps. She was a fucking wet dream come true. Her cheeks were tinted with a slight blush, her chest rising in fast breaths. With her naked like this, Rafe could see the slight swell of her stomach and he became impossibly harder. He needed to be inside her *now*.

Reluctantly, he tore his gaze from hers and looked at the floor in search of his pants. He needed to get a condom on before he lost his damn mind.

"Rafe, I'm clean."

He looked up at Sophie—was she saying he could fuck her raw? He'd never had sex without a condom, had never wanted to risk it. Now that the thought had entered his mind, Rafe wanted to fuck her with nothing between them more than he wanted his next breath.

"Thank fuck, I am too."

"Then what are you waiting for? It's not like you can get me pregnant *again*," she said with a wry smirk. Before she'd even finished her sentence, Rafe had returned to the bed, settling himself between her legs. His cock brushed her wet slit and he groaned, running his hands up her arms to join their hands.

Sophie squirmed under him and his cock head slipped into her entrance. Rafe kissed her gently, teasing her with shallow thrusts. She moaned in frustration and Rafe found himself smiling.

"What do you want, sweetheart? You sound frustrated."

"Fuck me, you smug bastard!"

Hearing the filthy words from her mouth, Rafe couldn't hold back anymore. He entered her in one hard thrust.

Fuck, I'm not going to last long.

Her tight heat wrapped around him and he couldn't recall a better feeling. He knew he would never get enough of her. He pulled all the way out before thrusting back into her.

"Oh fuck, Sophie. You feel so damn good."

Sophie groaned in response and Rafe let loose, pumping into her in uncontrolled thrusts. He took her hard and fast, his hips snapping into hers, the sounds of their fucking filling the room. He felt his balls draw up and knew he wasn't going to last much longer. He leaned down and kissed Sophie hard, his tongue fucking her mouth to the rhythm of his dick. When he felt her tight pussy clench, her heels digging into his ass, he knew he would be coming in a matter of seconds.

"Come with me, Sophie. Come on my cock," he gritted

out, sweat beading on his forehead as he fought to postpone his orgasm. He swiveled his hips, finding her sweet spot, and felt her orgasm sweep through her. As Sophie came, she bit his shoulder and he couldn't hold back anymore. He came with a shout, seeing stars as the most powerful orgasm he'd ever had rushed through his body.

Rafe collapsed on top of Sophie, his arms suddenly too weak to hold him. He'd never felt anything like that in his life, had never known sex could even be so mind-blowing. Realizing he was probably crushing her, he rolled to his side, pulling her into his arms as she kicked her heels off.

He pushed one hand through her hair, the other cupping her cheek. He loved seeing her like this, her eyes drowsy and sated, her cheeks flushed and lips swollen from his kisses. Rafe lowered his lips to hers, kissing her gently, reverently. He released her lips, kissing her cheek, her nose, and each of her eyelids. When she opened her eyes and smiled at him, he could feel his heart pounding, beating for her.

"Soph, that was—"

"Fucking incredible," she murmured, tucking her face into his shoulder. He ran his hands up and down her back, fingertips caressing her smooth skin.

Before nerves got the best of him, he spoke the words he'd been holding back all night. "I don't want just three dates. I want this—*us*. I want to give us a real shot."

She lifted her head and placed a hand on his chest over his heart. "You're just saying that because you're all sexed up and happy."

Rafe took her chin in his hand, kissing her lightly. "No, I'm not. I was going to talk to you about this at dinner, but the whole waitress fiasco kind of got in the way. I'm serious

—I don't want to just co-parent with you. I want to be with you."

Sophie shook her head. "That's the thing though, Rafe. Things like that will always happen. You're Houston's Finest. There are girls all over the city who are just dying to sink their claws into you. I don't know how to compete with that."

"There is no competition. You're all I see, Sophie. None of them matter to me."

She smiled and kissed him. "Let's talk after that third date, okay big guy?"

It wasn't the answer he wanted, but before he could argue further, Sophie's hand moved down his chest, slowly tracing his abs. Within seconds, he was ready for round two. Her hand moved down to his cock, and she stroked his shaft slowly.

Rafe's head fell back onto the pillow and he thrust into her hand. If she kept touching him like that, he'd spill all over his chest in minutes. He grabbed her hips and hauled her on top of him. Placing her hands on his chest, Sophie sunk down onto him, one excruciating inch at a time.

Two orgasms later, Rafe curled himself around Sophie's body, fitting her back to his front, and drifted to sleep. She didn't know it yet, but he wasn't letting her go.

CHAPTER TWENTY-ONE

SOPHIE WOKE up the next morning feeling deliciously sore. As it turned out, both she and Rafe were insatiable. They'd fallen asleep after their first two rounds of mind-blowing sex only for her to wake him up with a blow job. Before the sleep had even cleared from his eyes, he'd flipped her over for the slowest, most passionate sex she'd ever had. Just thinking about it had her ready for another round.

Rolling over, Sophie reached for Rafe on the other side of the bed only to find it empty. It was then that she heard sounds coming from her kitchen; she could make out the light chatter of James's voice followed shortly by a rumbling laugh from Rafe. She quickly dressed, throwing on a tank top and yoga pants, before making her way out of her room. Sophie followed the voices and found Rafe flipping a pancake high in the air before catching it in the pan.

James, comfortably seated in his booster seat, watched the path of the pancake, clapping and giggling when it found its home in the pan. Sophie leaned against the entrance to the kitchen, nothing short of entranced by this side of Rafe. He'd slipped on his dress pants from last night but left his upper body bare, his muscles flexing as he scooped one pancake out of the pan, laying it on a plate, before using a ladle to fill the pan again.

This comfortable scene was one that she could see herself waking up to in the future. James replaced by Rafe and Sophie's small child, his dress pants replaced with pajama bottoms. She fought the urge to stride across the kitchen and wrap her arms around his torso. One good date did not a relationship make.

If she were being entirely frank with herself, Sophie could admit that the ease of this *thing* with Rafe terrified her. He was a calming presence in her life, logical and stalwart, but easy to crack a smile. He said that she was giving him this, giving him a family, but it scared her to realize that he could give her the same thing. They could be more than co-parents if she let herself fall for him, for this relationship. Given the way their relationship had begun, however, she couldn't help but wonder where Rafe's feelings stemmed from.

While she was falling for him fast, he could be only giving this a shot because of the baby. Would he have ever pursued her, contacted her, if she hadn't gotten pregnant? Maybe he was only in this because he was trying to create the family he'd never had. Though she could understand his need for that, she wanted to be more than that, to be more than just the girl he'd gotten pregnant and ended up with. She could easily see Rafe becoming more than that for her, but what if he only stuck around for their baby?

She had seen what that kind of marriage could turn into. Her parents had gotten married young after her mother had gotten pregnant in college. Her father had been unhappy, but he had tried and tried to make the marriage work because he wanted Sophie to have a family. Their relationship had been tumultuous—constant fights and screaming when they thought Sophie was sleeping. Finally, when she was ten years old, her mother left and never looked back. Her dad had been devastated, not because he felt any love for her mother, but because he'd wanted Sophie to have two parents.

Initially, Sophie had been wary of Rafe because he reminded her of her exes. Rafe was attractive and he knew it; he'd been so damn cocky in their initial interview—an insufferable flirt. The more she got to know him, however, she realized that he must have been putting on an act. Sure, Rafe was attractive, but he didn't clamor for attention like Carlos. He actually seemed to abhor the minor fame he'd received as a result of the Instagram incident and her subsequent interviews. Any doubts she'd harbored about him in that aspect had been vanquished on their date last night when he'd shut down their waitress soundly.

She was pulled from her thoughts by a squeal of delight from James as Rafe pulled apart a still warm pancake, placing bite-sized pieces on the table in front of him. She stepped into the kitchen as though she'd just woken up and hadn't been watching the pair of them together. Naturally, Sophie headed straight for the coffee pot, which she was thrilled to see was full of piping hot liquid deliciousness. She reached for her usual mug and had begun to fill it with coffee when she felt strong arms wrap around her.

Rafe ran his nose up the column of her neck, giving her goose bumps, and planted a small kiss on the skin where her shoulder and neck met.

"Good morning, gorgeous." He nipped his way up her

neck to whisper in her ear as his hands drifted to her hips. "These yoga pants give me ideas, Soph."

Sophie let her head fall back on his shoulder, her coffee forgotten, and let out a small moan. "Four rounds weren't enough for you, big guy?"

Rafe practically growled into her ear, "I don't think I'll ever get enough."

The words gave Sophie butterflies, her earlier concerns resurfacing. She resumed her quest for coffee, filling her mug to the top and twisting out of his arms to lean against the counter and take her first sip. She eyed him over the top of the mug and saw a flash of confusion cross his features at her dismissal. Before he could question her, Sophie changed the subject.

"What's for breakfast?"

Rafe chuckled. "Well I got up to get you a cup of coffee and heard this little guy stirring in his crib. I figured you and Kelsey would want to sleep in so I grabbed him and brought him to the kitchen. Pancakes are my specialty, and I was already awake." He offered up a small shrug, as though getting James out of bed and cooking him breakfast were some small feat.

She couldn't help the smile that overtook her face. "Do I get pancakes too?"

Rafe nodded at the table, indicating that he wanted Sophie to take a seat. "Coming right up." He walked over to check on James, ensuring he had a full sippy cup and plenty of pancake bits in front of him, before returning to the stove to make Sophie's breakfast.

He looked at Sophie over his shoulder. "So what do you want to do today? Ramirez and I snagged a rare Saturday off."

Before she could come up with a response to his offer to spend the day together, they were interrupted by Kelsey's entrance. She shuffled slowly across the kitchen toward the coffee, rubbing the sleep from her eyes. Sophie and Rafe watched the coffee shuffle with amusement, waiting for her to notice that her son was already awake and fed. Kelsey had just lifted the mug to her mouth when James let out a displeased squawk, having apparently run out of pancake pieces.

He looked to Rafe, his tiny hands reaching as though he could grab the food straight from the counter if he tried hard enough. "More pancakes please," he said with surprising calm for a three-year-old. Rafe chuckled and obeyed, tearing up a few more pieces of pancake for him.

Kelsey's eyes widened, her gaze moving from Rafe to James and back again. "On a scale of one to ten, how horrible of a mother am I for not realizing my child was awake?"

Rafe let out a loud laugh before responding. "He woke up about an hour ago, but I grabbed him before he could wake you. Figured you could use a day to sleep in."

Sophie watched her best friend's jaw drop. "You...you got him up? I mean, you let me sleep in? What is happening right now?"

Rafe shrugged. "I'm sure being a single parent isn't easy, and I was already up."

Kelsey repeated his words dumbly, "You were already awake..."

"Want some pancakes?"

"You got my son out of bed *and* made us pancakes? Next you'll tell me you changed his diaper too."

"Well yeah." Rafe rubbed the scruff on his chin shyly. "Is

that okay? I mean I changed him from the diaper into the underwear on the changing table and took him to the bathroom. I noticed the little potty training toilet and made sure he used it before I put the underwear on. Is that okay?"

Kelsey looked like she wanted to leap across the kitchen and wrap Rafe in a hug. "Who the fuck are you? Superman?"

The moment the curse word passed her lips, Kelsey slapped her hand over her mouth, but it was too late. James had already plucked the bad word out of the sentence and was now chanting it through a mouthful of pancake.

At that, Sophie burst out laughing and Kelsey's head hit the table.

Once Rafe had made pancakes for the three of them, he set the plates on the table and joined them to eat. He entertained them with stories of Carlos during his first year on the force, which had Kelsey and Sophie laughing so hard they were crying.

"So he tries to pull his gun from his utility belt, and completely forgets to unclip the holster first. I'm telling the suspect to put down his knife and get on the ground, and the guy is obviously trying not to laugh. When I look over at Carlos, he has on what I'm sure he thinks is his serious cop face as he tries to yank the damn gun from his belt."

Kelsey howled with laughter, slapping the table. When they'd all managed to stop laughing, Kelsey stared at her plate, obviously feigning nonchalance as she asked, "So how is Carlos, anyway?"

Rafe snorted without looking up from his own meal. "You know Ramirez—working way too much and still sleeping his way through Houston's female population."

Kelsey visibly flinched at the words, and Sophie kicked

Rafe under the table. He choked on the bite he'd taken and shot Sophie a dirty look.

"What did I do now?"

Sophie sighed. "Nothing. So let's hear about your first year on the force."

Rafe grinned back at her. "I was goddamn perfect, of course. Best rookie Houston has ever seen, sweetheart."

After they'd eaten and cleaned up, Sophie and Rafe headed back to her bedroom. She wanted to spend the entire day with Rafe, but that was the problem. If she was already feeling attached after a night, what would an entire day in his company do to her? She needed to come up with something, anything, to get some space. Unfortunately, she was a terrible liar and Rafe happened to be a cop. Someone who was literally trained to detect lying in suspects.

Rafe walked into her bedroom like he owned it, scooping his shirt up off of the floor and looking to her as he buttoned it.

"I was thinking I'd run home and change and then you and I can do something? Maybe go to Kemah or Galveston?"

Sophie swallowed and shook her head slowly. "I have plans."

Rafe merely raised an eyebrow and continued buttoning his shirt, covering up the literal six-pack he'd obviously spent some serious gym time earning. He didn't look like he believed her even a little.

Shit.

"I, uh, promised my dad I would drive up to Austin to visit him today."

Rafe tilted his head. "A road trip to Austin sounds fun. I'd like to meet the grandfather of my child."

Of fucking course he would. She'd really walked right

into that. Rafe was looking at her as though he knew what was going on in her head. Hell, he probably did; the man was unnervingly perceptive. Knowing that Rafe wasn't one to mince words, Sophie figured she had a choice to make. Either she could take Rafe to meet her father, or she could have an honest discussion with him about her feelings. It wasn't a choice, not really. Sophie knew she wasn't ready to discuss her feelings, so it looked like she'd be going on a road trip instead.

Before giving in, she tried one last time to get out of this last minute adventure. "Don't you have to work tomorrow?"

Rafe shrugged. "Not until eleven at night. Ramirez and I are working graveyard tomorrow. I just need to be back around noon to catch some sleep."

Sophie sighed in defeat. "alright, let me shower and we can head to your place and grab some clothes."

At that, Rafe grinned triumphantly and began to unbutton his shirt again. She watched him hungrily as the muscles in his arms flexed and smooth; tanned skin became available for her perusal. When he reached for the top button on his pants, Sophie snapped out of the trance his body had put her in and looked up at his face.

"What are you doing?"

"You said shower, Soph. In this day and age, we really should conserve water. Plus, I've been *very* dirty for the last twelve hours or so. You really should wash me."

Sophie gaped at his words even as her body heated. She could feel the desire pooling in her core and clamped her mouth shut to hold in a moan as the mental image of Rafe's naked, wet body filled her mind.

She hadn't realized she was biting her lip until Rafe stepped closer to her, running his thumb over her mouth and practically growling, "Don't bite down too hard. I have plans for that gorgeous mouth. You have no idea how crazy you drive me, Sophie. No. Fucking. Idea."

Naked and aroused in front of her, Rafe ran his hands down her body, slowly peeling off her yoga pants and tank top. Unable to resist any longer, Sophie placed a hand on Rafe's chest, leaning up to kiss him. She'd meant for it to be a soft exploration, but the kiss quickly turned ravenous as he lifted her by her ass and wrapped her legs around his waist. They continued to kiss while he carried her into the bathroom, setting her on the counter and breaking their kiss to turn on the shower.

With the water warming up for their shower, Rafe pulled Sophie off of the counter and turned her to face the mirror, bending down to kiss and bite her neck while his hands found her breasts. Her head fell back as he tweaked her nipples, and a low moan slipped out of her. His lips moved to her back and he began slowly trailing kisses down her spine. Rafe's hands left her breasts and he used them to gently push her shoulders forward, bending her over the bathroom counter.

As his kisses trailed lower and his hands found her ass, Sophie realized where this was heading. At the first swipe of his tongue through her slit, she felt her knees buckle, the cool granite of the counter holding her up.

"You taste so fucking good, Sophie. Better than pancakes."

Rafe's hands were now exploring her body as he licked and sucked on her clit, and before long, she felt her orgasm building. He moved one hand to grasp her ass and slid two fingers from the other inside her. One gentle nip and soothing suck on her clit had her shattering, practically screaming his name as she came on his tongue. He continued to lick and stroke her through her orgasm, stopping only when she'd stopped shuddering. Rafe straightened behind her and pulled her into his body, his blue eyes meeting hers in the mirror as he licked his lips.

"Look at you, all flushed for me." He hummed in approval and grabbed her hand, pulling her into the shower with him. The water was warm and soothing, washing over her. Rafe stepped up behind her and began to lather shampoo into her hair. She could feel his hardness pressing against her, but he made no move to take care of himself.

Though she'd come moments ago, Sophie wanted more; she wanted to feel him fill her again. While Rafe massaged her scalp, she arched her back, pushing her ass against him and grinding. He sucked in a sharp breath, but continued washing her hair.

She stepped forward, pulling away from his body and tipped her head back to wash the shampoo out of her hair. Then, Sophie got down on her knees and in one swift move, engulfed his hard cock. Rafe groaned and fisted her hair, slowly pumping into her mouth as she sucked. She reached a hand up to cup his balls and had just begun to lave her tongue over the head of his dick, when he pulled her to her feet, kissing her fiercely, and once again wrapping her legs around his waist.

She was so wrapped up in the kiss that she barely registered the hard wall of the shower against her back before Rafe filled her in one thrust. He moaned her name and pulled out, filling her again in moments. He leaned his forehead against hers, their warm breath mingling as he set a furious pace.

"Fuck. Fuck, Sophie, you're so wet and warm and tight."

His breaths were coming more and more quickly as he pounded into her. She moved her hand between them and began rubbing her clit in slow circles, feeling her second orgasm building in her core. He looked down between them, watching himself fill her.

The sight of their joining shattered what remained of Rafe's control; his thrusts hurried. "Please tell me you're close. I'm not going to last much longer," he breathed, those bright blue eyes meeting hers.

The look in his eyes combined with the knowledge that she could make him lose control pushed her over the edge. Sophie's orgasm hit her hard and fast, her core clenching around his cock. Rafe's orgasm followed hers, and he bellowed her name as he filled her.

When Sophie came down, she and Rafe were both still breathing heavily. She smiled at him. "Conserve water, huh? I'm not even under the showerhead, Rafe. If anything, we're wasting water here."

He laughed in response and lowered her to her feet, her legs still a bit wobbly. "Hey, I just wanted to shower with you. You came on to *me*. I'm innocent in all of this."

Sophie slapped his chest lightly. "You are far from innocent, Officer Pierce."

"Keep calling me Officer Pierce and I may just have to pull out my handcuffs."

She felt herself flush at the words and imagined herself handcuffed to her bed, his body covering hers as he had his way with her. Rafe made her insatiable and she didn't know if she could ever get enough of him, of this. The thought terrified her.

CHAPTER TWENTY-TWO

RAFE CAME to a horrifying realization during their drive to Austin. Sophie had terrible taste in music. Fucking *terrible*. She made him listen to annoying ass pop songs the whole drive up, refusing to let him enjoy the classic rock he favored. By the time the Austin skyline came into view, he was close to ripping his own ears off and throwing them out of the window. Really, who the fuck didn't like AC/DC? The mother of his child, that's who.

Glancing across the car at his road-trip companion, he did have to admit that she looked pretty damn cute singing along to the abhorrent music she loved. She was staring out the window, her head bopping along to the song as she mouthed the words to some annoyingly up-tempo number. She'd rolled down the window, filling the car with the warm scent of summer in Texas. The wind blew through her hair, tossing the straight, blonde strands around.

After their shower adventure this morning, they'd gotten dressed, stopped by his apartment, and hit the road. The drive to Austin was easy and surprisingly beautiful, filled with lush trees and hills. When they weren't arguing over their music choices, they'd ridden in companionable silence. Rafe had been tempted to reach over the center console of the car to twine their fingers, but hesitated.

He'd known Sophie had almost blown him off this morning, claiming she was busy when he was sure she had no plans for the day. While Sophie had dressed, Kelsey pulled Rafe aside, thanking him again for breakfast and offering him some advice.

"Sophie is a little bit skittish. She's been cheated on by every serious boyfriend she's had. I guarantee she'll try to pull away, but if you stick it out, she'll cave. I see how you look at her, how she looks at you. It's rare and you should hold onto it."

Rafe's fists had clenched at the thought of anyone hurting Sophie. He'd almost asked Kelsey for the names of her exes, wanting to look them up and beat the piss out of them for daring to step out on her. Instead, he decided to thank his stars; those idiots must not have realized what they'd had in Sophie. He was reaping the benefits of their mistakes, and he would do everything in his power to earn her trust.

"Thanks, Kelsey. When you aren't shoving *The Greatest Showman* down my throat, you aren't so bad."

Sophie's best friend had grinned before her expression turned serious. "If you hurt her, all of the cops in your precinct won't save you. I will rip off your balls and fucking feed them to you."

Though tall, Kelsey was willowy and didn't look particularly fierce. However, the look in her eyes had him shuddering and cupping his manhood. He'd mumbled a bullshit excuse about needing to check his tire pressure before leaving the house. Waiting for Sophie outside had seemed like the safest option.

Sophie indicated that it was time for him to exit the freeway, directing him to a subdivision in the northern part of the city. He wasn't sure what to expect from her father; she'd been surprisingly tight-lipped about her family. She'd mentioned a father, but had never given any indication that she had a mother. Maybe, like his, her mom had died when she was young? He could ask her about it later. For now, he needed to focus on charming the shit out of Sophie's father.

Sophie's directions led Rafe to a modest brick house in a cul-de-sac. It was obvious that her father took good care of the home; the grass was lush and freshly trimmed, the driveway clean. He tamped down his nerves and grabbed his and Sophie's overnight bags from the trunk of his car before following her to the front door. Instead of knocking, as he'd expected her to do, Sophie pulled her keys out of her pocket and unlocked the front door. She called out for her father, and Rafe tailed her through the comfortable house to the back patio where a man in his fifties sat with an iPad and a cigar. He put out the cigar as soon as he'd spotted his daughter and stood to pull her into a big hug.

"Pumpkin! What a surprise! I wasn't expecting you this weekend."

Sophie shot Rafe a guilty look before responding. "I *did* tell you I would visit you this month. I just didn't specify *when*."

He grunted and turned his gaze to Rafe. His expression was steely as he took in the man who'd gotten his daughter pregnant. Rafe found himself straightening his spine and reaching out a hand. "Rafe Pierce, sir. It's a pleasure to meet you."

Sophie's father huffed and took Rafe's proffered hand. "So you're the charmer who knocked my daughter up, huh? You gonna marry her?"

"Dad! You can't ask people that."

"This is my house, pumpkin. I do as I damn well please."

Rafe released Mr. Klein's hand and replied honestly. "I think the practice of getting married because of pregnancy is a bit antiquated, sir. For now, I'm happy to just date Sophie and raise our child."

Surprisingly, Mr. Klein cracked a huge smile. "Good man. You want some whiskey? And none of that 'sir' bullshit either. Makes me feel like I've got one foot in the damn grave. You can call me Jim."

Rafe nodded. "Well in that case, Jim, I think I'd love some whiskey."

Shit, Jim could hold his liquor. Two hours, countless tumblers of whiskey, and a cigar later, Rafe was hammered. He and Jim had bonded over their shared hatred of the Dallas Cowboys and their love of classic rock. It turned out Sophie's dad had recently retired after working as a VP of Marketing for most of his life. He also happened to be a former military man and loved that Rafe was a police officer. The sun had set about an hour ago, and Sophie had gone inside at the mention of cigars. Rafe, who'd been planning to turn down Jim's offer to smoke with Sophie around, had happily accepted the offered Cuban once Sophie had left.

When Rafe looked up from lighting his cigar, he was met with Jim's steely green gaze. He wasn't sure why, but it was obvious that the tone of their conversation was about to change.

"I hate to sound like the clichéd father here, but I have to ask. What are your plans with Sophie?"

Rafe sputtered, a little bit more intoxicated than he'd planned to be for this conversation with Sophie's father. He set down the tumbler of whiskey and tried to sharpen his thoughts. This conversation was important; the last thing he wanted to do was mess it up.

"Well, we didn't have the easiest start, honestly, and after that night in the bar—"

Shit, he hadn't meant for that to slip out. He now understood why Jim had been refilling his damn glass all night. He'd wanted to loosen Rafe's lips. No father wanted to hear about his daughter's one-night stand with a near stranger, but Rafe wasn't sure how to recover from his slip up. He shifted awkwardly in his seat, and Jim laughed.

"I know how babies are conceived, son. Just move past the awkward."

Rafe sucked in a breath and started again. "To be honest with you, I was kind of a prick to her. She was prying into my life for that damn story, and I wanted nothing to do with it. So I shut her out as best I could. Now though," he paused to collect his thoughts.

"I'm realizing that you have an incredible daughter, one I could easily see myself falling for. Hell, there's a damn good chance I'm already falling. She keeps trying to push me away, but I want to fight for us to have a shot at this, at being a family."

Jim hummed, taking a long sip of his drink before responding. "Being co-parents doesn't make you any less of a family. If you're only with Sophie because she's pregnant, I can tell you right fucking now that it isn't going to work out."

"You speaking from experience, Jim?"

At that, Jim barked out a laugh. "Hell yes, I am. I married Sophie's mother because she was pregnant. We both had pretty strict, by-the-book parents, and marriage was just expected. To say it was a mistake would be putting it mildly. Sure, we liked each other well enough, but if she hadn't gotten pregnant, we would have fizzled out and gone our separate ways. Ten years of built-up frustration blew up in the worst possible way. Sophie's mom left us and never looked back. I've spent years wondering what would've happened if we had just decided to be friends. Sure, Sophie's life would have been different, but she'd have a mom around, you know?"

"I don't think it's fair of you to put that all on yourself, Jim. She didn't just leave you; she left Sophie too. A good mother wouldn't have done that, regardless of the state of her marriage."

Jim waved a hand, pushing aside Rafe's words. "What I'm trying to say here is that if pregnancy is what you're basing your relationship on, it's going to fail. Spectacularly."

Rafe considered, taking a long drag from the cigar in his hand. The conversation had sobered him up, and his thoughts came clearer. "Sophie isn't just the mother of my child. She's smart as hell and sharp-witted. That girl keeps me on my toes and makes me laugh like nobody else can. When she walks into a room, it's like all of the air has been sucked out of my lungs. Not because she's beautiful, though she is, but because that's what her presence does to me. I know she and I will make great parents, even if we aren't together. But I want to try with her because I've never felt this way about anyone before."

Jim whistled low. "I feel like this is the part where I'm supposed to say 'If you break my daughter's heart, I'll break your neck,' but I'm sure Kelsey's already taken care of that threat for me."

Rafe laughed, remembering how fierce Sophie's best friend had been. "Her threat was a bit more graphic than yours actually."

"Good. I'll say this instead: my girl won't make it easy for you. She's dated some real pieces of shit. I swear, that fiancé of hers couldn't take his eyes off of his own damn reflection long enough to notice Sophie. If you want an actual relationship with her, she'll make you work for it. Be prepared."

Rafe nodded. "It wouldn't be worth it if it was easy."

"Good man. Now stop being a pussy and pick that drink up. We have half a bottle to kill, and I wanna talk about the Texans playoff chances this year."

Rafe lifted the tumbler, offering Jim a small salute before taking a large sip of his drink. "Well JJ Watt looks pretty fucking good, but defense isn't really our issue. What we need is a take-charge QB and an offensive line that knows how to form a damn pocket."

Rafe woke up the next morning with a pounding headache, some serious morning wood, and a hot, half-naked

Sophie in his arms. Her ass was tucked into his groin and she was using his arm as a pillow. After he and Jim killed the bottle of whiskey, he'd stumbled to the guest room, only to discover Sophie had put them in separate rooms. He'd debated for all of ten seconds before entering the room she'd chosen for herself and crawling into bed beside her. He didn't want to sleep alone when she was so close.

Headache forgotten, he ran his hand up and down the side of her body, caressing her waist and hips. He circled his hand around her body and found the small baby bump she tried so hard to hide. It was quickly becoming his favorite part of her body to touch. Aside from her boobs maybe, and her ass. If he was honest with himself, he was a walking erection and would prefer to keep his hands on her body at all times.

Rafe left his hand on Sophie's abdomen and began to lightly kiss her cheek before working his way down to nuzzle her neck. She was so warm and soft in the morning. He nipped her shoulder and couldn't resist the urge to grind his erection into her ass. Sophie stirred and groaned sleepily.

"You know you're supposed to have your own room, right?"

Rafe hummed against her neck, slipping his hand down to cup her over her panties. "Sleepovers are no fun without a late-night panty raid."

She protested even as she arched into his touch, her eyes still closed. "We are at my dad's house, Rafe."

"Well then I guess you'll have to be really quiet when you come on my tongue in a few minutes."

"You're awfully sure of yourself, Officer."

Rafe bit her earlobe gently. "Are you saying you don't think I can make you come, Sophie?"

She shrugged, and Rafe grinned wickedly into the curve of her neck. "Challenge accepted." Not giving her a chance to respond, he rolled her onto her back and settled between her legs to get to work. When Sophie's moans began to fill the room, he was at least gentlemanly enough to give her a pillow to stifle the sound with.

CHAPTER TWENTY-THREE

STANDING in front of the mirror in her old bedroom, Sophie dropped the towel she'd dried off with after showering and took in the changes this pregnancy had put her body through. Her breasts were definitely swollen, something she knew Rafe was enjoying. She placed her hands on the ever-growing bump she'd come to love so much. She couldn't believe she was almost eleven weeks pregnant. Her little baby was now the size of a fig, and in five short weeks, she would know if she and Rafe were having a boy or girl. She felt a smile form on her lips as she thought of Rafe's reaction. He would be thrilled either way—she knew that—but he definitely seemed to want a boy. If their little peanut ended up being a girl, Sophie had no doubt Rafe would want to try for a boy next time.

Next time? What the fuck, Sophie?

She wasn't even sure they were dating. They were doing something, but she needed to keep her distance. Co-parents. That was all they could ever be. She had only brought him with her to Austin because she figured her dad would want to meet the father of his grandchild. This was not the next step in a relationship; she needed to remember that.

Sophie threw on her favorite yoga pants, with sheer cutouts running down the sides, and a comfortable off-the-shoulder shirt. She padded to the kitchen in search of Rafe and her dad. The latter was sitting at the kitchen table, drinking a cup of coffee and reading the paper. He looked up when she sat down across from him, his glasses on the tip of his nose, coffee cup halfway to his mouth.

He took a big gulp of black coffee and smiled at Sophie. "Mornin', pumpkin. Rafe went to the store to grab eggs for breakfast. Did you sleep well?"

"Best sleep I've gotten in a while actually. It's hard to get comfortable when my back is always aching. I didn't think I was far enough along for back pain." She'd been struggling to stay asleep for the last few weeks, waking up in the middle of the night to back aches or random cravings. Last night, however, she'd slept like the dead, wrapped up in Rafe's strong arms. A blush stained her cheeks when she thought of the wicked way he'd woken her up.

Her father chuckled. "The look on your face tells me you didn't sleep alone. That boy is smitten with you, ya know?"

"Hardly. He's just around because I'm having his child. He's always wanted to be a father."

"Go ahead and tell yourself that, pumpkin. I don't believe for one second that Rafe is the kind of guy who would stick around if he didn't want to."

Sophie knew her father spoke the truth. Rafe wasn't the kind of person who would do anything he didn't want to do. That didn't mean that he wanted to stay for the right reasons though. He was so excited to have a child; the woman giving that to him was bound to be on the receiving end of his affection—for a while at least. How could she ever know that Rafe was with her for *her* and not just their child?

"I see those cogs working, Soph. Give him a chance. He's got a good head on his shoulders. I like him much more than I liked that idiot chef you brought around."

Before she could respond, she heard the front door open, indicating Rafe had returned from the store. She wondered what he would make them this morning; was French toast too much to ask? He placed the groceries on the kitchen counter and bent down to kiss her cheek. With no makeup or bra on, and with wet hair, she was sure she looked like a mess, but Rafe took in her appearance leisurely, as though savoring it.

"Looking beautiful as ever, babe. How do pancakes sound?"

Though she smiled at the term of endearment, Sophie tried to keep her shoulders from slumping in disappointment. She knew it was ridiculous to be sad she was getting pancakes instead of French toast, but her cravings had been out of control recently. This baby liked sweets apparently.

"Pancakes sound great, Rafe."

Rafe bursted out laughing. "Oh Soph, your face is priceless right now. If you don't want pancakes just tell me what you want and I'll make it."

"Awfully sure of yourself, Officer. What if you can't make what I want?"

Rafe scoffed, "Try me."

"Fine, I want eggs benedict," she replied, throwing out the most challenging breakfast dish she could think of.

"Hmm, I don't think I grabbed everything I would need for a hollandaise, but the store isn't far. I'll be right back."

Was he for real? She was tempted to let him go to the

store just so she could see what her dad really thought of him. He'd been sexy as hell making pancakes the other day, and those were relatively easy to make. When he grabbed his keys and started to head back to the front door, Sophie stopped him.

"Rafe! I was kidding. You don't have to go to the store. I'm sure we have the ingredients to make what I want." She rummaged through her dad's kitchen, locating the items she knew were needed to make her favorite breakfast meal. She'd tried once a few years ago to make it and had ended up completely ruining her skillet and burning the food to a crisp. Locating the bread in the pantry, she grabbed cinnamon, nutmeg, and finally the milk from the fridge. She pulled the eggs out of the bag Rafe had brought in and procured a large bowl, skillet, and spatula as well. Rafe approached from behind, looking over her shoulder at the ingredients.

"French toast, huh?" He kissed her bare shoulder. "Go sit down, I've got this."

Sophie returned to the table and was met with a smirk and raised eyebrow from her father. She'd almost forgotten where they were, too wrapped up in Rafe to remember anyone else existed. Her dad took a sip of coffee and cleared his throat.

"So you cook often, Rafe?"

Rafe shrugged. "When I have the time, yeah. It gets expensive to eat out every day, especially on a patrol officer's salary. Learning how to cook saves me money and helps keep me healthy. Unless I'm cooking for Sophie, of course."

Before Sophie could defend herself, her father laughed. "So is she still eating pie for breakfast, lunch, and dinner?"

Sophie said *no* at the exact moment Rafe said *yes*. She

shot him a glare across the kitchen, the traitor. He blew her a kiss and chuckled, turning back to his cooking.

After they'd eaten breakfast and cleaned up, Rafe and Sophie had said goodbye to her father and hit the road. It was still pretty early in the morning, but Rafe needed to get in a workout and a nap before he worked that night, so the sooner they returned to Houston, the better. She spent the drive home contemplating her morning: the way Rafe seemed to fit into her life so seamlessly. Her dad didn't like many people, had never liked a single one of her exes, but wholeheartedly approved of Rafe.

She certainly couldn't deny that he was a great guy—different from her exes in every way imaginable, and although she knew it was irrational, she just couldn't shake her fear that something would go wrong. She was falling for Rafe against her better judgment, and she never wanted him to feel trapped like her dad had. Sophie needed some time away from him to think things over. When they returned to Houston, she would take a couple weeks to work through her emotions and come to a definitive decision. It wasn't fair of her to be so wishy-washy with him.

When they were about thirty minutes outside of city limits, passing the Kickapoo exit that always made Sophie snicker, Rafe's phone rang through the Bluetooth in his car. She saw Carlos's name pop up on the screen and reached across the center console to push the accept button on Rafe's steering wheel.

"Hey! I was going to ignore that call, Sophie."

Carlos's voice came through the speaker system. "Wow, real nice, fucker. Ignoring your partner in his time of need."

Rafe scoffed. "Time of need? You're such a drama queen."

"This is absolutely my time of need, man! I'm in a bit of a situation. I went home with this girl last night, and today when I tried to get some morning nookie, I guess I called her the wrong name."

Sophie snorted. "Keeping it classy, as always."

"I can feel your judgment through the phone line and I'm not amused, shortcake. *Anyway*, this chick kicked me out and I didn't have time to grab my wallet, keys, or clothes. My phone is about to die and I can't call an Uber while I'm naked. I need you to come get me. I'm hiding in the damn stairwell at her apartment complex and I'm sure her neighbors will call the cops on me if they find me. The last thing I need is *another* naked incident for the guys at the precinct to laugh over."

Rafe laughed. "What do I get out of this though?"

"Dude! Now is not the time to fuck with me. I will tell Sophie about the strip—"

"Text me the damn address, asshole," Rafe replied before hanging up. "He wasn't about to say *strip club*. He was talking about a strip, um…" He scratched his head, clearly searching for an acceptable way to end that sentence.

Sophie quirked an eyebrow at him, trying to hide her smile at his obvious discomfort.

"Yeah, there isn't really any way for me to recover from that one, huh?"

Sophie laughed. "He backed you into a corner, big guy. Give me your phone. I'll put the address he sent you into your GPS."

In the past, when she'd asked her exes for their phones, they'd made up excuses or opened their phones to the screen she needed. Rafe, however, handed his phone to Sophie without a moment's hesitation, telling her the password to unlock it. She quickly plugged in the address and directed him to the apartment complex. Carlos's hookup lived in a high-rise building in the Galleria area. Within minutes of them pulling up, Rafe's partner came barreling out of the front door, naked as the day he was born. He wasted no time, jumping into the car quickly.

"I thought you were hiding in the stairwell. How did you see us pull up?" Sophie asked, her curiosity getting the best of her.

Carlos sighed. "The doorman caught me in the stairwell, when he was walking the property, and had me come downstairs to wait. I was hiding in the lobby bathroom, and he knocked when you got here."

"Only you, man. Only you would get yourself into this predicament."

"Hey! In my defense she had a really weird name. She yelled it at me when I was running out of her apartment. It was like Italian or something, I don't know."

Sophie shook her head. She couldn't believe this was the guy her best friend was pining over. Sure, Carlos was hilarious, and he'd always been kind to her, but he also seemed determined to fuck every woman in Houston. She must've scoffed out loud without realizing it, because Carlos stopped his conversation with Rafe to lean forward and look at her.

"What was that about, shortcake? I sense some judgment here."

"I just don't get it—how can you sleep with a different woman every night? Wouldn't you rather actually date someone?"

Carlos shrugged, his bare shoulders lifting. "If the right

girl doesn't want to be with me, I don't see the harm in sleeping with a few of the wrong ones."

Assuming he was talking about Kelsey, Sophie couldn't keep the snark out of her tone when she replied, "Well maybe the right girl just doesn't want to catch syphilis from one of the hundreds of girls you're fucking."

Instead of getting frustrated or argumentative with her, Carlos sat back in his seat. "I could be celibate and it wouldn't change a damn thing. Besides," he grumbled, "it's not *hundreds*."

Sophie took pity on him and changed the subject. For the remainder of their drive to his house, she and Carlos talked about the Astros World Series chances this year. When they pulled up in front of his home, Rafe hopped out of the car and unlocked the front door with the spare key Carlos had apparently given him. When the door was wide open, Carlos leaned forward, pecked Sophie on the cheek, and bolted for the door. She laughed at the sight of his bare ass running up the driveway and into the house.

CHAPTER TWENTY-FOUR

SOPHIE WAS AVOIDING HIM. Rafe had felt her pulling away on their drive back from Austin three weeks ago. He'd tried to make plans with her when he dropped her off at home after leaving Carlos's house, but she'd claimed to have plans. Work had been busy as hell and he'd wanted to give her time to work through things on her own, so he'd stayed away. He had continued to text her and still had pie delivered to her house at least once a week, but he hadn't pushed her to see him. He understood that she was skittish, especially after hearing about her parents' relationship, but he was done staying away.

He hadn't slept for shit without her in his arms, and he was sick of jerking off in the shower like a fucking teenager. He also found himself missing her smile, her wry sense of humor, and her aversion to healthy food. After a long day of work, he wanted nothing more than an easy night in with Sophie. When he'd tried to make plans with her earlier today, Sophie had blown him off once again, this time saying she had plans with Kelsey. Naturally, he'd done what he had to, pestered Carlos for Kelsey's number and enlisted her help. Sophie's best friend had been more than happy to help him get his foot in the door, so to speak.

Rafe smiled as he walked down the sidewalk toward Sophie's house. He had parked around the block so that she wouldn't see his car, not wanting to give her another chance to run for it. The meal he'd purchased hung from his fingertips, the bag swaying gently as he walked. Sophie would be getting home from work in about thirty minutes, and he was going to be at her house with dinner and a movie waiting when she walked in the door.

Kelsey let him in and followed him to the kitchen, peeking in the bags he'd brought. "Oh, Italian food, huh? I did mention that I would accept payment in the form of delicious food, right?"

Rafe slapped Kelsey's hand when she reached for the baguette peeking out of the top of the takeout bag. Reaching into the bag, he grabbed one of the to-go containers and handed it to her. He'd gotten her fettuccine alfredo, always a safe bet when ordering Italian food.

"Consider yourself paid in full, Kels."

"Excuse you? I help you break into my best friend's house, tell you what time she's coming home from work, and agree to hide in my room for the night, and I don't even get any damn bread? Rude, Rafe. Fucking rude."

Rafe sputtered in response, "I fed you, woman!"

"Yeah, Italian food without bread. I feel cheated. Cheated of delicious carbs."

He sighed and pulled the baguette out of the bag, handing it to Kelsey dejectedly.

"Oh, Rafe. I'm fucking with you. I mean, I do take bread very seriously, but I'm not going to steal my pregnant best friend's dinner. That's just asking for it. I tried to steal a grape off of her plate the other day and she looked like she wanted to stab me."

Before Rafe could respond, he heard the front door of the house opening. Kelsey snagged her food and a bottle of wine from the fridge before running down the hallway toward her room. Sophie had come home earlier than he'd expected and he hadn't even had time to get the food on plates. He could hear Sophie moving through the entry of the house, kicking off her shoes by the door and putting her purse down on the small table there.

"Kels? Are you home? My feet are fucking killing me. I was thinking we could get pedicures and then come home and eat our weight in chocolate."

Rafe stepped out of the kitchen and took Sophie in. Shit, he'd missed her. Her long hair was pulled into a knot at the top of her head, and she was wearing a green button-down tucked into a gray pencil skirt. The skirt was high-waisted and showed off the little baby bump she was currently sporting. His heart pounded in his chest at the sight, and he fought the urge to get on his knees and kiss the bump containing his growing baby.

He leaned against the doorway to the kitchen and crossed his arms over his chest. "So those are your exciting plans, huh? You blew me off for a pedicure and chocolate?"

Sophie's eyes widened before narrowing on Rafe. "Oh I'm going to kill Kelsey. She let you in, didn't she?"

"Oh yeah, she sold you out for some fettuccine alfredo."

At the mention of food, Sophie visibly perked up. "You brought food?"

Rafe nodded. "I did. You can only eat it if you'll hear me out though. I know you're avoiding me and we have some things to discuss. I gave you three weeks of space; now it's time for you to let me talk."

Sophie at least had the decency to look sheepish. "Fine, but this better be some damn good food."

He couldn't contain his laughter—of course that was her main concern. If he were completely honest, the upcoming conversation had him more than a little nervous. If all went well, though, he'd make sure to rub her feet tonight. He'd read that swollen feet was common when pregnant, and those sexy heels she wore constantly couldn't be helping anything.

She passed him and waltzed into the kitchen, wasting no time and pulling the containers of food out of the bag quickly. She inspected them, choosing the pasta he'd purchased with her in mind before grabbing a fork and settling at the table. Rafe grabbed his own food and drink and joined her. Sophie was already eating her meal by the time he sat down, and she groaned in satisfaction, the sound going straight to his dick.

Down boy, you'll get your turn later.

He tried to take a bite of his food, but hardly tasted it as he chewed. He needed to say what he'd come to say before he could relax enough to enjoy his meal.

He cleared his throat and launched into the small speech he'd prepared on his way here. "So I know that you're scared, Sophie. Your dad told me about his relationship with your mom, and I am so sorry that you had to go through that. I need you to know this, though: I don't want to be with you because you're pregnant. We could be fantastic co-parents, and if you can honestly say that you have no feelings for me, I'll accept my lot in your life. I will be here for you and our baby no matter the outcome of this discussion. I just want to make sure that you're aware of my feelings.

"I didn't have an easy childhood. When my mother overdosed and I was taken into foster care, I didn't even know my own name. She had always called me Boy, and my father wasn't in the picture. The police didn't find a birth certificate for me in the tiny apartment we shared, and the social worker assigned to my case was unable to locate my birth records. I actually chose my own name, Raphael, after my favorite Ninja Turtle. I chose my last name because the police officer who found me was named Pierce Johnson. I've never had a family; it has always been just me. Nobody knows that story. I haven't even told Carlos."

Sophie had put her fork down, and her eyes swam with tears. Thankfully, there was no pity in her gaze, only sad understanding. "Oh, Rafe." She shook her head. "I can't imagine going through that."

"I won't lie and say it was easy, it wasn't. I'm telling you this so that you understand how important our baby is to me. Honestly, us dating could really make this complicated. I can't predict the future, and I don't know how this will work out for us. You need to know first and foremost, though, that I will never, *never* abandon you or our child like your mother did. I also won't put you through a relationship that you don't want just because we have a child together.

"All of that being said, I do want to be with you. We could do this separately, share custody and expenses, stay friends, and deny what we are feeling. I'm alright with that, but it isn't what I want. You're giving me a family no matter what, and I'm so incredibly grateful, but I don't want to raise this child without you. I want to wake up with you in my arms; I want to be here to fulfill your insane cravings at all hours of the night; I want to make you smile and laugh. I'm falling for you, and I want this to be a relationship."

Rafe got out of his chair, abandoning his food completely to kneel in front of Sophie. "I'm all in, Sophie. It won't always be easy, and building a relationship with a baby on the way is probably stupid, but I want this. I want you."

Tears were streaming steadily down Sophie's face now. He honestly wasn't sure if it was a good or bad sign, but he really hoped she'd take this leap with him. He'd meant what he said, though: if she didn't want a relationship with him, he wouldn't push it.

Sophie wiped the tears from her eyes and placed her hand on Rafe's cheek. "I'm scared, Rafe. Relationships have never gone well for me. I have a terrible track record with men. But, I'd be lying if I said I didn't have feelings for you too."

Rafe nodded, not quite sure what to say. His heart was pounding as he waited for her to say the words he wanted to hear.

Sophie smiled, and it lit up the room. "This might be the dumbest thing I've ever done, but I'm all in too, Rafe."

His hands were in her hair and his lips were on hers before she could take her next breath. He hadn't realized how terrified he was of her answer. Rafe had never been great at relationships, always hesitant to open up, always worried women would hear about his past and think of him as tainted goods. It hit him with a startling clarity how much he wanted to be with Sophie, how much this meant to him.

He put as much reverence into his kisses as he could possibly manage, showing her without words how glad he was that she was taking a chance on them. Rafe kissed her slowly, softly tangling his tongue with hers as his hands massaged her scalp. When he finally pulled away, he leaned his forehead against hers and laughed.

"I didn't even need all three dates to convince you. Damn, I'm good."

Sophie slapped his chest lightly, pushing him away. "I take it all back, you cocky bastard."

Rafe lifted his eyebrows and winked at her. "Oh, am I cocky? Tell me, Soph, just how *cocky* am I?"

Her lips twitched as she tried to hold in her laughter, and she returned to her meal, pointedly ignoring him now. That just wouldn't do. Rafe stood up and leaned over her chair. He bent down and nipped at her earlobe before kissing his way down her neck. It had been three long weeks without her, and his dick was harder than rebar just thinking about sex with Sophie. She tilted her head, giving him more access as he continued to kiss and bite his way down her neck.

Rafe grabbed Sophie's hand and placed it over the bulge in his pants. "Cocky enough for you, babe?"

Sophie groaned. "You fucking tease." She began to stroke him through the thick material of his jeans, and he knew he could get off from that slight touch alone. He needed to be inside her as soon as possible. Fortunately, it appeared Sophie felt similarly. She stood up and took his hand, leading him into the bedroom where she closed and locked the door before dropping to her knees.

The sight of her there, on her knees in front of him, made his dick twitch. He sucked in a harsh breath, but kept his hands at his sides, allowing her to take the lead. When Sophie looked up at him and licked her lips, reaching for the button of his jeans, he knew that he never wanted this to end.

CHAPTER TWENTY-FIVE

SEVENTEEN WEEKS PREGNANT

PREGNANCY BRAIN WAS the literal worst. Sophie searched her room again for her purse. She could've sworn she'd brought it into her room last night after work, but it was nowhere to be found now. Her doctor's appointment was in fifteen minutes and her fucking purse was missing. Thankfully, she had her phone so she called Rafe; maybe he could come pick her up.

He answered on the second ring. "Hey, babe. Are you almost here?"

Sophie tried to keep the hysterics out of her voice, but she knew she sounded panicked. "No, I'm not on my way. I can't find my fucking purse, and my damn jeans don't fit so I'm going to see my doctor in fucking yoga pants. I'm fat and forgetful and I can't find anything in this stupid house."

"Whoa, slow down, Sophie. Take a breath for me, okay?"

Sophie rolled her eyes. Taking a breath wasn't going to help her find her fucking keys. She opened her mouth to tell him so, but he was already telling her to breathe in. Sophie took a deep breath and held it until he told her to release.

She did this three more times at his urging and she slowly felt the panic begin to leave her body. She placed a hand on her continually growing belly.

"Feeling better?"

Sophie sighed. "Yes, that helped. But I still don't know how I'm going to make it to our appointment, Rafe."

"Alright, one thing at a time. How's our little avocado today?"

She couldn't stop the smile that overtook her face; every week Rafe referred to their baby by the fruit or vegetable he/she was closest in size to.

"She's fine. According to the book she might start kicking soon. And did you know that she can hear us now?"

"Sounds like I'll have to read *him* some books tonight so he can get used to the sound of my voice."

"You can read *her Harry Potter*. I've been wanting to reread anyway," she said with a laugh.

Sophie could hear the smile in Rafe's voice when he replied, "You got it, babe. Our son will be a *Harry Potter* fan. Now, tell me what you did last night when you got home."

"I got home, grabbed some ice—fruit, some fruit from the fridge, and got into bed."

"Fruit, huh? What flavor was the ice cream? I'm betting you had Half Baked."

She sighed. "You know me too well."

Rafe laughed. " You say that like it's a bad thing. Go check the freezer for your purse."

There was no way she'd left her purse in the damn freezer. She was forgetful, not stupid. People only did that kind of shit in books or movies. Nevertheless, Sophie made her way to the kitchen, humoring him and checking inside the freezer.

"It's not—oh."

"Find it?"

Sophie pulled her purse out of the freezer with a huff. "Nobody likes a know-it-all, Officer Pierce."

"You fucking love it. See you soon, Soph. I'll tell the doctor you're running a few minutes late."

She hung up the phone and shoved it into her ice-cold purse, pulling her car keys out and making her way out of the house. As she drove, she thought about the last few weeks with Rafe. They'd spent almost every night together since they'd decided to become a real couple three weeks ago. She'd given him a key to her house for the nights he got off work late, slipping into bed and wrapping himself around her. She loved falling asleep in his arms every night and waking up to his handsome face every morning.

He'd taken her on a few more dates, each one more fun than the last. None of their dates were the standard fare—he took her to mini golf, to the Kemah Boardwalk (where he won her an embarrassingly large stuffed moose), and even to an evening of Shakespeare in the Park.

When she pulled up to the doctor's office ten minutes later, Rafe was standing outside waiting for her. He walked over to the car as she got out, taking her purse from her and helping her out of the car.

She could get out of the car without help, of course, but Rafe had been treating her like breakable china since he'd found out how badly her back was hurting recently. Last week he'd surprised her with a hot bubble bath after work. The memory of his hot body behind hers, massaging her shoulders and gently washing her, brought a blush to her cheeks. They hadn't even dried off completely before falling onto her bed, and she'd had to change the sheets and comforter that night before they went to sleep.

Rafe took in the heat in her face and tilted his head. "Now what are you thinking about that has you all red?"

Sophie shrugged. "I was watching *Thor* last night before bed. I was just thinking about naked Hemsworth brothers."

He hummed, wrapping a hand around her waist and pulling her body into his. Her breasts met his chest and he placed a hand on her neck, gently tipping her face up. Rafe kissed her softly, his tongue caressing the seam of her lips, seeking entrance. When Sophie opened for him, Rafe swept his tongue into her mouth once before pulling back.

"You're a terrible liar, Soph. And your purse is fucking freezing."

She laughed, pushing him away. "Come on, you insufferable man. We have a doctor's appointment to get to."

She'd called the office earlier this week and found out that if the baby was cooperating, they could determine the sex today. Sophie hadn't told Rafe yet, wanting to surprise him. He thought this would be a standard checkup and ultrasound appointment. She couldn't wait to find out what they were having and was looking forward to the look on Rafe's face. He was so sure they were having a boy, but Sophie was hoping for a girl. It had become a running joke with them, arguing daily over the gender of their child.

They'd been waiting in the exam room for a few minutes when the ultrasound technician walked in to greet them.

"Are we ready to find out the sex of the baby today?"

Rafe looked at the technician with wide eyes before turning to glance at Sophie. "Today? Did you know? We're finding out today?"

Sophie laughed at the excitement in his expression. He

looked positively thrilled, and she was glad she'd kept this surprise from him.

"Yep! Today our little avocado becomes a boy or a girl!"

The tech looked between the two of them, a grin forming on his face. "Lie back for me, Sophie. We'll get the ultrasound started now."

She leaned back against the exam table, paper crinkling loudly behind her. The tech rubbed cold gel on her stomach before placing the probe over her uterus. He moved it around for a few moments before an image formed clearly on the screen. Rafe reached down and squeezed Sophie's hand as the sound of their baby's heartbeat filled the room. It was one of the most perfect sounds Sophie had heard in her entire life.

She looked at the ultrasound screen and was astounded to see a tiny human; there were little arms and legs, and she could even see the baby's ears. Rafe leaned down and kissed her on the top of her head. When she glanced up to take him in, the love on his face as he looked at the screen took her breath away. Nobody deserved to be a father more than Rafe.

The tech moved the wand around a bit more and then asked the big question. "Alright, are y'all ready?"

"We have bets on this, buddy. Please tell me you see a little penis on that screen," Rafe said with a smile at the tech.

The tech laughed and winced. "Well, I hope you didn't bet too much money, man. You're having a girl."

Rafe sucked in a sharp breath, staring at the screen a few moments longer before turning to Sophie. There were tears in his eyes, matching the ones in hers. He leaned his forehead against hers, placing one hand on either side of her face.

"A girl, Soph. We're having a fucking daughter."

Sophie leaned in to kiss him softly. "You're going to be wrapped around her tiny finger. I just know it."

He laughed, a breathy sound. "I think I'm already wrapped around her mother's finger."

Looking into his blue eyes in that moment, bright with tears and so much hope, Sophie knew. She was head over heels in love with Rafe, and she never wanted this to end. It was the most terrifying thought she'd ever had.

After an emotional day, Sophie couldn't wait to spend a night in with her girls. Following their doctor's appointment, Rafe had gone to work, leaving her evening free. It was cult classic night and *10 Things I Hate About You* was the movie selection of the evening.

She'd gone to the bakery after her doctor's appointment and placed a rush order for a special cake to surprise her friends with. It had cost her a pretty penny at the last minute, but it would be so worth it. Though she couldn't drink anymore, she'd also picked up a few bottles of wine for her girls, earning her a glare from the bag lady at the grocery store. Sophie had almost told the girl to fuck right off, but had instead smiled and wished her a nice day.

Sophie had just set out the chips and queso she'd picked up from El Tiempo, their favorite Mexican restaurant in the area. She'd also gotten fajitas and, of course, guacamole. It had been a while since she'd had a cult classic night. Between her crazy work schedule, Kelsey's messy divorce and custody issues, and Rafe, the timing just hadn't been right in a while. Tonight though, Rafe was working, and James was with his father.

She heard the front door open and peeked her head into the entry of the home she shared with Kelsey. Her two best friends were shucking their shoes and purses.

"Well, well, well. Look what the cat dragged in."

Becky looked around pointedly. "Umm, I see pussy, but there are no cats here."

Sophie let out a loud laugh before running to greet her friend. "Shit, I've missed you."

"Likewise, bitch. Look how big you're getting! In a few months I will be the only person in our friend circle whose vagina hasn't been stretched out by a baby."

Kelsey slapped Becky's shoulder. "My vagina is *not* stretched out. Kegels are a wonderful thing, my friend."

Sophie shook her head and moved into the living room. She took a seat on the sectional, pulling the bowl of tortilla chips into her lap. She was starving, and had been craving chips and queso for days. At this point, she honestly wouldn't mind just a straight spoonful of queso. Kelsey went to the kitchen to grab wine glasses for her and Becky while Becky opened one of the bottles of red Sophie had purchased. Kelsey handed her a glass of ice water, poured the wine, and sat in her usual chair. Becky plopped down on the couch next to Sophie, swiping a handful of chips to eat with the guacamole she'd pulled into her own lap.

Sophie turned on the movie and waited for her friends to grill her. She knew it was coming; it was only a matter of time. Sure enough, before the opening credits had finished, Becky turned to face her on the couch.

"So, what's going on with you and Rafe?"

Sophie shrugged, but couldn't keep the dopey grin off of her face. "We've been dating for a few weeks now. He's intimidatingly perfect, if I'm being honest."

Becky nodded seriously. "Ah, so he's got the perfect cock."

Kelsey laughed, causing the first spit take of the evening.

"Son of a bitch, Becky. I swear you wait until I have wine in my mouth."

"I'm here to ask the important questions! How many inches? Ten? Eleven?"

Sophie looked at her friend in alarm. "Ten inches? Are you fucking kidding me? That just sounds painful. Like I'm pretty sure I'd take one look at a ten-inch cock and nope the fuck out."

Kelsey nodded in agreement. "I mean, can you imagine trying to give head to a guy with a dick that huge? I can just see my obituary 'Death by Big Dick.' It's not how I want to go."

Becky shrugged. "You really just need to have lube and do some prep. As for blow jobs, use your hands ladies, use your hands."

Laughing, Sophie replied, "I think your sex life would kill me, woman."

"I have done some pretty fun shit. Oh, I was reading a romance book the other day, and the guy put grapes in the woman's vagina. It kinda sounded fun; I'm curious about it."

Kelsey's eyes widened comically. "I'm sorry, did you just say grapes? In her vagina?"

"Yeah! He like rubbed them on her clit and then just slipped them in."

Sophie jumped in. "Please, please tell me he took them out? That just seems really unsanitary."

"He popped them and then fucked her."

Kelsey did another spit take, reaching for the paper towels on the table before speaking up. "That just can't be safe. I don't think I'd ever be able to do that. He'd put them in there and I'm pretty sure I'd tell him to put his damn hand in and pull them out."

Sophie nodded in agreement. "And then I'd kick his kinky ass out."

Shrugging again, Becky replied, "Y'all are missing out. Big dicks and food play are where it's at."

"I'm not opposed to food play, actually. When Carlos and I—" Kelsey broke off the sentence, seeming to realize what she'd just admitted.

Sophie hadn't heard Kelsey talk about Carlos in weeks. She knew that he'd spent the night at their house a few months ago, but Kelsey rarely brought him up. "When you and Carlos did what?"

Kelsey blushed and took a big gulp of wine, pointing at her cheeks to indicate she couldn't speak with a full mouth.

"You can't hold that wine in your mouth all night. I'm sure you know the importance of swallowing."

Kelsey rolled her eyes and swallowed, a blush staining her cheeks as she slowly answered. "Okay, okay. We slept together once. There may have been some strategically placed whipped cream involved. No big deal."

"Now I bet he's good in bed," Becky replied. "I saw him dancing on my birthday. That man knows how to move his hips."

Kelsey clearly didn't want to talk about Carlos anymore and changed the subject. "Did you know that in ancient Egypt, servants were slathered with honey to keep flies away from the pharaoh?"

Sophie laughed at her friend's diversion. Kelsey had a habit of spouting off history facts when she was nervous, something Sophie found both boring and endearing. At least this fact was interesting. Instead of responding, or pushing further, Sophie turned to Becky.

"I have a follow-up question for you, Becky. Who the hell

have you been with that had a ten-inch cock? I know for sure it wasn't that asshole you dated last year. Ricky, or whatever his name was."

Becky's face paled a bit and she took a steadying gulp of wine before responding. "Yeah, no. Ricky was good with his tongue, but he was disappointing downstairs. You guys remember, um, Reese?"

Sophie felt her jaw clench. "Ugh, of course that piece of trash would have a nice dick."

Reese had been Becky's high school sweetheart, and to say that their past together was troubled would be an incredible understatement. If Sophie ever saw that fucker again, she'd lay him out flat.

"You haven't heard from him or anything, have you?" Kelsey asked cautiously.

Becky shook her head. "No, the last I heard, he was living in Dallas."

At just the mention of Reese, Sophie's brash, confident friend had fallen silent, a contemplative look overtaking her features. Sophie clapped her hands and stood.

"Ladies, I think it's time for the cake!"

"I'm all about cake," Kelsey said, "but what is the occasion? I wouldn't be surprised if you pulled out pie...but cake?"

Sophie smiled. "Well, Rafe and I went to the doctor's office this morning, and we got some news. News that had me rush-ordering a cake with a color-dyed interior."

Her friends looked confused for a moment, not picking up on Sophie's hint immediately. She saw the moment Becky realized what she was talking about, her face lighting up as she jumped from the couch. "You know the sex of the baby? Get that fucking cake, woman!"

She laughed and stood up to grab the cake from the fridge, snatching a few plates from the cabinet, and spoons and a cutting knife from the drawer while she was at it. When she walked back into the living room, the expectant looks on her friends' faces were almost comical. Apparently they were as excited as she was. She placed the cake on the coffee table, setting the plates and utensils next to it. Kelsey and Becky looked at each other, coming to some silent agreement, before Becky picked up the knife to cut into the cake.

She'd gone simple: the cake was covered in delicious white buttercream frosting and had a strawberry-flavored interior. She was almost as excited to eat it as she was to share it with her friends. Kelsey squealed when Becky began cutting into the cake, the pink of the sponge becoming almost immediately visible.

Within seconds, Kelsey and Becky's arms were around her in a group hug so cheesy it could rival a Disney movie. She didn't care though; these two girls meant more to her than anyone in the world. When they pulled away, she realized Kelsey was crying.

"You realize what this means, right? Our kids are *so* getting married. James will come to accept his arranged marriage eventually."

Sophie laughed. "Kels, you've been reading way too much romance. Betrothals are not a thing anymore."

Becky, never one to stay out of a conversation involving romance novels, jumped right in. "Hey, I just read a series set in modern times with a betrothed couple."

Kelsey shot Sophie a look that clearly said, *See? I'm always right.*

"The main character was a demon, though, so I'm not a hundred percent sure that counts."

Sophie sighed, feigning exasperation. "You two are impossible. This is proof that you'll turn literally any conversation into a romance novel discussion."

Her friends both scoffed, and Becky rolled her eyes. "You are just as much of a romance fiend as we are, woman."

"This is so off topic it isn't even funny." Kelsey laughed. "You're having a girl! We will be sure to raise her on cult classics and romance novels."

"Is there any other way to raise a child?" Sophie asked, keeping her face as serious as possible before bursting out laughing.

Becky returned to the cake, cutting them each a slice and serving it on plates. When they were all seated and eating, Becky turned to face her on the couch.

"So, tell me. How are things with Rafe, really? Is he excited to be a father? Are you two serious? How's the sex?"

Sophie laughed, taking a bite of cake to give herself a moment to think before answering. "He really is incredible. It all feels too good to be true, and I'm just waiting for the shit to hit the fan. I've never had a successful relationship in my life; there is no way I just stumbled into one now. And the sex is out of this fucking world. Hands down the best I've ever had."

"He seems to be pretty serious about you, Soph. I know your exes have been awful, but I'm really proud of you for giving this a shot," Kelsey replied, reaching over to squeeze her hand.

"I'm pretty sure I'm in love with him. It's fucking terrifying. My first instinct is to run for the hills, you know? This would all be so much simpler if he was just some guy I was dating, but a ruined relationship with the father of my child? What if he doesn't love me, or he cheats, or we break up for any number of other reasons? We will still be in each other's lives forever."

Becky jumped in, stopping her from rambling further. "Alright, let's say you didn't date him. Let's say you ended it now and you two just raised this child together. Eventually, he's going to date someone else, maybe even get married. Can you honestly imagine seeing him start a life with another woman? Because you *will* see it. Your daughter ensures you'll have a front row seat. Can you handle watching that happen, knowing that you lost your chance with him because you were scared? People break up, Sophie. It happens. But if you end things before they really start, I guarantee you'll regret it."

"I've seen you two together, Sophie," Kelsey said. "He looks at you like you're his whole damn world. Having been here through all of your dating mishaps, I can say with complete certainty that he is nothing like anyone you've dated before."

Sophie mulled over their words and imagined seeing Rafe with another woman. Her chest hurt at the thought of him touching anyone but her, giving someone else his silent comfort, his sleepy smiles. She rubbed at the pain in her chest as though that could ease the ache. Her friends were right—she didn't want to be with anyone else, and she sure as hell didn't want Rafe with anyone else.

Her phone rang from the coffee table, startling her from her thoughts. When she saw Rafe's name on the screen she smiled. Cult classic night was sacred, though, and she wasn't about to break their cardinal rule: No Dicks Allowed. Before she could reach over to silence the phone, Kelsey picked it up and swiped to answer.

"Hey lover boy, when are you getting your sexy ass over here?"

Becky and Sophie burst out in laughter, and then watched as Kelsey's face flushed brightly. "Oh, hi, Carlos. Why are you calling Sophie on Rafe's phone?"

Her friend sucked her bottom lip between her teeth. "Oh, right. Yeah, she told me the news. Did you know that women in biblical times gave birth standing on two bricks? They were called birthing bricks."

Sophie needed to save her friend immediately; who knew what kind of random history she'd spout if left on the phone with Carlos much longer. She stood and reached over to grab the phone from Kelsey's ear, putting it to her own instead.

"Hey Carlos, what's going on?"

"Not much, shortcake, just learning about birthing bricks —a pretty standard night for me."

Sophie laughed. "So I'm guessing Rafe told you the news, yes?"

"We're having a girl! Should I go pick up a shotgun now? Uncle Carlos is gonna have to chase the boys away somehow."

"I'm sure you and Rafe will come up with some way to keep boys away from her. Speaking of, is Rafe there?"

"What, my conversation isn't scintillating enough for you? I'll grab him for you, but I'm fucking offended, Sophie."

She rolled her eyes, but chuckled when she heard Carlos through the now muffled phone line. If she had to guess, she'd say he was covering the speaker with his hand and yelling across the room at his partner.

"Hey, Officer Pencil Dick! Your baby momma wants to talk to you!"

She heard a shuffle and a muffled, "Fuck, man, that hurt," from Carlos before Rafe's smooth voice came through the line.

"I'm going to fucking murder him. He just yelled that shit across the damn precinct. Everyone in roll call heard him." Rafe growled.

"I mean, you could always whip it out and prove him wrong."

"Why, Ms. Klein, I'll have you know that's considered indecent exposure."

Sophie blushed and turned her body away from her friends, not quite wanting them to hear what she said next. "You could just indecently expose yourself to me instead," she whispered.

"Dammit, Sophie, I've told you how uncomfortable it is to get hard in these fucking polyester pants. I'm about to leave work now. Can I come over?"

Sophie turned back to her friends, taking in the half-eaten Mexican food, the cake, and the cult classic still playing on the TV.

"I can't tonight. It's cult classic night. Chicks before dicks and all that."

Before he had a chance to respond, Becky pulled the phone from her hand. "Sophie will be at your place in thirty. Dress sexy." Becky listened to Rafe's response and disconnected the call, throwing the phone across the couch at Sophie.

"Dear Lord in heaven, that man's voice gets me all kinds of hot and bothered," she said, fanning herself.

"What the hell, Becky? I can't ditch you guys on girls' night."

"Sure you can." Kelsey shrugged. "Maybe you could grow a pair and say the L-word to him tonight. Or, you could just *indecently expose yourself.*"

Sophie threw the small pillow next to her across the room, nailing Kelsey in the head. "You're the actual worst. I need new friends."

Becky reached over and shoved her lightly. "Get your ass up, woman. We're officially kicking you out."

Sophie chewed on the inside of her cheek. She didn't want to ditch her friends, but she did really want to see Rafe. Plus, they were practically pushing her out the door. "We've never stayed at his house before, and I've only been there once. I didn't even go inside, and I definitely don't remember how to get there."

"Good thing he's going to text you his address then," Becky replied. "Stop making excuses and get your fucking ass over there."

Sophie held her hands up, "Fine, fine." Becky slapped her ass as she walked by, and she grinned. She really did have the best friends.

CHAPTER TWENTY-SIX

SOPHIE PULLED up to Rafe's building, parking in one of the spots indicated for visitors. It was a gated complex, so she called him as she got out of her car, heading to the main entrance. The apartment building was all brick and was surrounded by a wrought iron fence. She pulled open the large gate and ascended the stairs leading to the small, gated doorway to get into the actual complex. He picked up on the second ring and said he would be down to let her in in just a moment.

A few moments later, she saw him walking toward her, sweats slung low on his hips and a tight athletic T-shirt hugging his upper body. She felt her core clench and her nipples pebble in her sports bra. She'd like to blame her intense reaction on pregnancy hormones, but she knew it was just him. Rafe was mouthwateringly sexy, and she found herself wanting him day and night.

He opened the gate and let her in, grabbing her hand and pulling her into his body to plant a quick kiss on her lips.

"Hey gorgeous," he murmured, his lips brushing hers a second time.

Before she could sink into it, he pulled her through the complex's courtyard toward the stairs. The building was beautiful—two stories of apartments looking down on a pool and barbeque area in the center of the courtyard. They walked up to the second story, and Rafe led her to an apartment with a dark-stained wooden door.

He opened the door and gestured for her to walk in before him. His apartment had hardwood floors and a warm, masculine feel. It was decorated in grays and blacks, with a large leather sofa and flat screen television. Before she could inspect it further, she felt something furry brush across her legs. Sophie jumped in alarm, gripping Rafe's arm tightly.

He laughed and bent down to pick up an orange ball of fluff. "Sophie, this is Socks. I swear, he's harmless."

"You have a cat?"

"Hey, what's so shocking about that? I don't like to come home to an empty apartment, and I'm not home nearly enough to have a dog. I started feeding Socks a few years ago; he was just a stray in the neighborhood," he said, rubbing the cat under his chin. "He decided to stay here with me, and the rest is history."

Sophie's heart clenched at his words. Of course he didn't want to come back to an empty apartment; he wanted a family to fill his home. This man continued to surprise her at every turn. She reached over and let Socks sniff her fingers carefully before petting him. After a few moments, he apparently decided he'd had enough and jumped out of Rafe's arms, tearing across the apartment like his tail was on fire.

Rafe reached for Sophie's purse, placing it on the couch

and lacing his fingers through hers. "Do you want the full tour?"

"As long as this tour ends in your bedroom, I'm in."

He shook his head. "Really, Sophie. I'm more than a piece of meat, you know."

She rolled her eyes and followed him through the apartment. He kept it clean, and she wasn't the least bit surprised to find his fridge fully stocked with healthy food. Not a pudding cup or slice of pie in sight. They reached a closed door and he stepped behind her, placing his hands on her hips and kissing her shoulder lightly.

"I think you should open this door first, babe."

Sophie threw a confused look over her shoulder before twisting the doorknob and pushing the door open. What she saw in the room took her breath away. It was a fully furnished nursery. She stepped over the threshold into the room, flipping the light switch on as she went. There was a plush gray rug on the floor, and a dark wood crib was pushed against the far wall. The window was already fitted with a blackout curtain, and he had purchased a dark wood changing table and rocking chair to match the crib. She noticed that the walls were bare and wondered if he had plans for those. Now that they knew they'd be having a daughter, she could picture this room filled with pale pink to complement the grays.

She turned around and found Rafe leaning against the doorjamb, a soft smile gracing his lips. Sophie walked across the room and wrapped her arms around him, placing a gentle kiss over his heart.

"When did you do this, Rafe?"

"Well, I moved into a two-bedroom unit as soon as I found out you were pregnant. I've been kind of furnishing the room over the last few weeks. I didn't want to do too much until we knew the gender. I thought maybe you'd like to help me decorate the room?"

She stood on her tiptoes and brought her lips to his, kissing him before pulling back to look into his clear blue eyes. "I would love to help you decorate it. Maybe we can go get some stuff tomorrow morning?"

A blinding smile took over Rafe's face. "That sounds nice." He paused, cupping her face in his hands, his eyes flicking over her face. He swallowed before continuing, "I know you have your house, but James and Kelsey are taking up your spare bedrooms, and I'm not sure what your plans are there. Maybe if we're at that point when the baby comes, you'd consider moving in here? With me? I know it isn't a house, but it's pretty spacious and I think we could be happy here for a few years. At least until I can afford to put a down payment on a house for us."

"You already think of these things?"

"I know how I feel about you, Soph. This is still pretty new and I won't rush you, but I know that I want to wake up with you and our daughter every morning."

She wasn't sure she was ready to live with him just yet, but she was open to discussing it. She was just barely into her second trimester, so they had some time to think things through. She was willing to admit to herself that she loved him, but moving in was a huge step. The last time she'd lived with someone, she'd come home to find him fucking another woman. It was hard to move past that, but she did need to come up with a plan before the baby was born. She knew Kelsey wasn't ready to leave just yet, and she certainly didn't want to displace James. The poor little guy was going through enough changes right now.

"I think it's something we can talk about."

Rafe smiled broadly before grabbing her by her hips, pulling her into the warmth of his body. She placed her hands on his chest, one over his heart, and looked at him. The warmth in his eyes threatened to steal her breath; the depth of her feelings for this man both terrified and thrilled her. He was caring, thoughtful, and he made her laugh on a regular basis. She'd never been in a relationship that felt this *easy*.

She didn't realize that she'd dropped her gaze until she felt Rafe's hand under her chin, tilting it up so that he could take in her features.

"Where'd you go?"

She smiled softly. "I was just thinking about how right this feels. I've never been in a relationship that felt this easy."

Rafe gasped and clutched a hand to his chest. "Are you calling me easy? I'll have you know I'm still a virgin."

Sophie raised her eyebrows and moved his hand to her stomach.

"So this was divine intervention, huh?"

He rubbed his hand over the baby bump before dropping to his knees. He kissed her stomach lightly a few times.

"You are already so loved, little girl. I can't wait to meet you, hold you, and spoil you. Your mom says I have to read you *Harry Potter*, so you'll probably come out a little nerdy, but that's okay—your mom's nerdiness is one of the things I love about her."

Sophie sucked in a sharp breath at the sound of the word *love* on Rafe's lips. Was it possible he felt the same way she did? The words were on the tip of her tongue when she felt movement in her womb. Rafe gasped, placing his other hand on her stomach.

"Sophie, did you feel that? Did she just kick?"

Sophie laughed and joined him on the floor, placing one hand on the growing bump. "Keep talking, Rafe. I want to feel that again."

"Alright my little avocado, want to hear a secret? I haven't even told your mom this one yet." He looked at Sophie, his dimple making an appearance as he offered her a small smile. "I am hopelessly, ridiculously in love with your mother. I love everything about her: her addiction to pie, her dry wit, her smile, her infectious laugh, and her abysmal cooking. You know, even first thing in the morning, without any makeup on, she is the most gorgeous woman I have ever seen. In seventeen weeks, the two of you have become my whole entire world."

Tears were streaming down Sophie's face by the end of his declaration, and she laughed when she felt her daughter kick again, responding to the sound of her father's voice. Rafe's laugh joined hers, his lips smiling against hers, as he leaned in to kiss her.

"You don't have to say it back if you aren't ready. I just couldn't wait another minute to tell you. I love you, Sophie. So damn much."

Sophie shook her head, grinning at him like a fool with tears still running down her cheeks. His thumb swept across her face, catching her tears and wiping them away. "Of course I love you, Rafe."

"You do?"

She nodded, her throat too clogged with emotion to continue speaking. He leaned forward and peppered her face with kisses, his lips touching her cheeks, her nose, and her forehead before finding her lips. Their kiss quickly turned carnal, his tongue meeting hers in broad strokes. He moved a hand into Sophie's hair while the other moved to cup her ass, pulling her into his body where she could feel his erection pressing against her stomach.

"Say it again," he growled against her lips.

Sophie pulled back, placing a hand on either side of his face and meeting his blue gaze. "I love you, Rafe Pierce."

His lips took hers again and he backed her into his bedroom, not stopping until she felt the backs of her knees touching the mattress. He slowly stripped them of their clothes, kissing her slowly, passionately the entire time. When he pushed into her, he pulled back to look into her eyes.

"Sophie," he said her name softly, reverently. He made love to her unhurriedly, his hands running over her body, tracing her curves as he brought them both to the brink of pleasure and pushed them over. When they climaxed together, he whispered words of love in her ear, his words and body bringing her to the most intense orgasm of her life. Sophie fell asleep that night wrapped in his arms, the sound of his heartbeat filling her ears.

CHAPTER TWENTY-SEVEN

RAFE WOKE UP SLOWLY, the previous night coming to him in pieces that made his heart feel as though it would burst at any moment. Sophie loved him. It honestly seemed too good to be true, and he couldn't imagine his life getting any better than it already was. His body was curled around Sophie's, and he placed his hand on her stomach. Not only had his daughter kicked last night, she'd kicked for the first time at the sound of his voice. He had never been so content in his entire life, and he could say with absolute certainty that it was all because of Sophie.

He loved that she challenged him, made him laugh, and made him want to be a better man. He'd never been a particularly open person, preferring to keep his past hidden. He knew that he'd done nothing wrong, but he had always been embarrassed of his childhood. His parents hadn't wanted him, none of the foster parents he'd been placed with wanted him; he'd never been chosen to be a part of a family. Now, though, he was making his own family, with Sophie.

She made him want to tell her everything, all about his

difficult past. He didn't have any deep dark secrets, just a childhood filled with abuse and neglect that he'd worked hard to forget. He was determined to keep his child from experiencing the same thing. She would grow up in a happy home, filled with joy and laughter and parents who loved each other.

Overwhelmed by the depths of his emotions, Rafe moved Sophie's hair and planted a gentle kiss on her neck, trailing his lips down to her collarbone and over her shoulder. She stirred in her sleep, a happy hum escaping her throat as he worshipped her. Though he'd had her only hours ago, he already wanted to be with her again. His cock twitched when his attention elicited a small moan from Sophie. He ground his erection into her ass and moved his hand up to cup one of her breasts, tweaking her nipple gently. In response, she pushed her ass into him, the pressure on his cock forcing a groan from him.

He was just starting to move his hand down to her delicious pussy when a shrill ring broke the silence of his apartment. He kept his phone on "do not disturb" at night, meaning only his captain, Sophie, and Carlos were able to get through to him.

"Rafe," Sophie moaned, "don't you dare answer that fucking phone. I need you."

He rolled Sophie onto her back, settling himself between her legs before leaning in to kiss her slowly. He stroked her tongue with his own and reached a hand between their bodies, his fingers searching for her wet heat. His phone stopped ringing only to begin again moments later.

"Fuck, babe. I have to get it. It could be the captain."

Sophie growled at him when he pulled away, causing him to chuckle. It was nice to know she was as ravenous for him as he was for her. He couldn't imagine ever getting enough of Sophie. He padded naked to the living room where he'd left his phone last night and swiped to answer when he saw his captain's name on his screen.

"This is Pierce."

"Rafe, get your ass down here. We need to have a discussion."

"Yes, sir. I'll be there in thirty."

His captain disconnected the call without responding. Returning to his bedroom, Rafe stopped short at the sight that greeted him. Sophie had kicked the covers off of herself and had two fingers in her pussy. Her eyes were closed, her head thrown back as she touched herself. His dick, which had deflated rapidly at the sound of his boss's voice, hardened painfully. Shit, this woman would be the death of him. He needed to take a shower and get to the station, but he couldn't let her get herself off when he was right here. He stalked to the bed and pulled her hand away from her mound. Her eyes opened, filling with lust at the sight of him. He took the two fingers that had been inside her and sucked on them, groaning at the taste of her arousal.

Sophie sucked in a breath, her chest rising and falling rapidly. Rafe climbed over her onto the bed, his naked chest covering hers. He kissed a path up her neck and lightly bit her earlobe.

"You don't come in my apartment without me, understood, Sophie?"

She nodded in response and he pulled away, kneeling between her legs and stroking his cock from root to tip. Her eyes followed the movement of his hand as he moved his dick to her pussy. He rubbed the head along her slit, circling her clit, biting back a moan at the wetness he found there.

"You goddamn tease, fuck me already."

Rafe laughed and lined his dick up with Sophie's heat. He pushed just the head in and she inhaled sharply.

"You want to come, sweetheart?"

Sophie moaned in response, and though he wanted to tease her, he couldn't hold back any longer. He snapped his hips, fully entering her in one broad stroke.

"Fuck, Sophie, you feel so damn good. I'm not going to last long."

"Then you'd better make me come quickly, Rafe."

He smiled at the challenge in her words and set a brutal pace. The sound of their bodies coming together filled the room, and he reached down to thumb her clit. He was already close, and the sight of her full breasts bouncing in time with his thrusts was enough to send him over the edge in a matter of seconds. He pulled one of her legs up, placing it on his shoulder and changing the angle. Within five strokes, he could feel Sophie's pussy pulsing around him, her orgasm coming on rapidly.

"Come with me, baby. I want to feel you come all over my cock."

His dirty words seemed to push her over, and he felt her wet heat clench around him, sending him into oblivion with her.

Rafe made it to the station with minutes to spare. He'd only had time for a quick shower before throwing on some jeans and a T-shirt and running out the door. Fortunately, traffic was light and he lived relatively close to the precinct, so the trip didn't take long. He walked through roll call, saying quick hellos to his fellow officers, and headed into the captain's office. The door was open so he walked in and took a seat.

He smiled, remembering the last time he'd been called into this very office. He'd been so sure that the interview and feature were the worst things that could happen to him. He never imagined he would be glad to have been mistaken for a stripper by a drunken bachelorette party, but he was. All of the publicity, the stupid emergency calls from women wanting to nail Houston's Finest, the name-calling at work — it had all been worth it for the woman currently sleeping in his bed.

Rafe wasn't sure why he was being called in for this meeting, but he hoped it wouldn't take long. He planned to stop and get Sophie a slice of her favorite pie before heading home. He would feed it to her in bed and then maybe go for round two.

Captain Stevens cleared his throat, pulling Rafe from his thoughts and bringing him back into the present.

"I got a call this morning from the homicide department, Pierce. How do you think your interview went?"

Rafe met the captain's eyes, confused. "I thought it went pretty fucking well, but it's been weeks and I haven't heard anything. I assumed they'd chosen someone else by now."

"Well, Sergeant Walters was impressed with you, but you're still pretty new to the force. He wanted a few weeks to vet you for the position, look closely at your time here."

Still not sure where this was heading, Rafe responded slowly. "Okay," he said, drawing out the word.

"Long story short, son, they want to offer you the job. I told them that I thought you were ready, so don't fuck this up. Don't want you to make me look bad."

Rafe's mouth fell open. "Are you serious? You look serious. Holy shit."

Captain Stevens laughed. "Yeah kid, you've earned this. You're one of the hardest workers I have. I'll be sorry to see you go. I need you to stay on until I find a good partner for Ramirez." The captain rolled his eyes. "He's good, but he's definitely a handful. It may take me a few weeks."

"Of course, I'll stay on as long as you need. Ramirez is a little bit of a princess, but he's a damn good partner."

Captain Stevens nodded. "I know. Anyway, congratulations, Detective."

"Thank you, sir. Can I head out?"

"Go ahead and enjoy your day off. Expect to meet with me and Sergeant Walters on Monday morning to discuss the details and your training."

He walked out of the precinct feeling like everything in his life was finally just as it should be. Knowing his partner would want to hear it from him, he dialed Ramirez through the car's Bluetooth on his drive home.

His friend answered on the third ring, "What's up, dick breath?"

Rafe chuckled. "I have some news, man. You're not gonna like it."

"Oh shit, who'd you get pregnant now?"

"Very funny, you're fucking hilarious. I just had a sit-down with the captain and—"

"He finally fired your ass? You really are the worst

partner. Remember that time you tried to pull out your gun but it was still strapped into your belt?"

Rafe sighed. "That was you, dumbass."

"Nah man, I'd never do something that fucking stupid."

"Carlos! I have actual news, man. News that impacts you."

"Well, spit it out already. You really do talk too much."

"I made detective. Homicide is giving me the job."

There was a long silence on the other end of the line and Rafe winced, thinking maybe he should've waited to tell Carlos the news in person. He was about to break the quiet when his partner's voice finally came through the speaker.

"Shit, Rafe. I'm so fucking happy for you, man. You deserve it."

Rafe let out the breath he didn't realize he'd been holding. He was going to miss working with Carlos every day, and had been nervous as hell to break the news. He should've known his best friend would be supportive. He always was.

"Thank you. I feel bad for the sucker they pick to replace me. You're a goddamn handful to work with."

Carlos scoffed, "You're out of your damn mind. I'm the literal best. You were lucky to have me for so long. So what are we doing tonight? We need to have celebratory drinks, naturally."

"Let me check in with Sophie, see what she's up to tonight."

"Woooow, you're fucking whipped, pretty boy."

Rafe smiled. "I sure as shit am. I'll text you and let you know what she says."

The first thing he smelled when he walked back into the apartment was something burning. He followed the smell into the kitchen and stifled a laugh when he saw Sophie standing at the stove, trying to stir clearly burnt eggs in the pan and cursing up a storm.

"Stupid fucking chicken fetuses. How hard is it to cook eggs? Dammit."

He moved as silently as he could, standing behind her and wrapping his arms around her waist. She was wearing one of his T-shirts, the hem sitting low on her body, just covering up her fine ass. Sophie jumped in his arms and hung her head.

"Looks delicious, babe. What are you making me?"

Sophie grumbled, "You're a damn liar, Rafe Pierce. It looks like burnt ass eggs. I was trying to surprise you with breakfast."

"Mmm, well you did manage to surprise me."

Sophie turned from the stove, her arms circling his neck, her hands winding into his hair. She gave him a quick kiss on the lips before pulling back.

"How was your meeting? What happened?"

Rafe couldn't contain the smile that broke out. "I got the detective job!"

Sophie jumped up, wrapping her legs around his waist and hugging him tightly. He shifted his hands to her ass, holding her against him. She pulled back and peppered kisses all over his face.

"I'm so proud of you, Rafe. You deserve it."

He laughed. "Fuck yes, I do. Years of partnering with Ramirez has finally paid off. Speaking of, he wants us to go out and celebrate tonight, but I wanted to see what you were up to first."

"Go celebrate! I'll stay in and work on some copyedits. I'm a little behind from taking off yesterday for the doctor's appointment. It'll be nice to catch up before I go back to work Monday."

"Shit, you're perfect." He kissed her, and what was meant to be a quick peck on the lips turned into a passionate tangle of tongues and teeth. He released her ass and Sophie slid down his body, rubbing against his erection on her way down. Rafe leaned his forehead against hers, his breath coming out in pants. He was on fucking fire for her.

"How about we start celebrating right now?"

Sophie quirked an eyebrow. "What about breakfast? I'm cooking for you, remember?"

Rafe growled and picked her up, carefully tossing her over his shoulder to avoid causing her and the baby any discomfort. He turned the stove off and pulled the now ruined pan off of the burner.

"I can think of other things I'd rather have for breakfast," he replied before hauling her off to the bedroom.

CHAPTER TWENTY-EIGHT

THE BAR CARLOS had chosen was loud and crowded, music pounding through the speakers as Rafe took another swig of his beer. He wondered how long he'd need to stay to avoid offending Carlos. He loved his best friend, but he would much rather be at home with Sophie. He imagined her on the couch in yoga pants and a big T-shirt, working on copyedits while she watched *The Greatest Showman*. The image made him smile, and he longed to leave this place, drive straight to her house, and pull her into his arms.

He pulled out his phone again, checking to see if she'd texted him. He knew she was probably trying to let him enjoy his night out, but he couldn't get her off of his mind. He was just unlocking his phone to text her when his friend punched him in the shoulder.

"Put that shit away, man. You're supposed to be celebrating with me."

Rafe sighed heavily and put his phone back in his pocket. Carlos was right—he was being a dick. Determined to make an effort to enjoy his night, he waved the bartender over and ordered a round of shots for the two of them. When the bartender placed the shots of whiskey in front of them, Rafe held his glass up.

"To years of putting up with your diva ass finally paying off."

Carlos laughed. "To you, Rafe. You're going to be the best damn homicide detective out there."

"Fuck yes, I am," he replied, tossing the shot back.

A few beers and countless shots later, he was fucking hammered. He and Carlos had started reminiscing, talking about their most disastrous arrests, while throwing back Jameson shots like they were water. He had to admit, he was having fun, but he wasn't entirely sure he could stand on his own at this point. He knew he needed to call an Uber soon; there was no way in hell he could drink much more. He patted Carlos on the back and headed off to find the bathroom. When he returned to his friend at the bar, he was unsurprised to see Carlos surrounded by women.

He was about to tell his friend he needed to leave when one of the girls squealed in delight, "Carlos, this is your partner right? Holy shit, Houston's Finest indeed."

She sauntered over and draped her arms around his neck. His thoughts were fuzzy, but he knew she wasn't Sophie, and he didn't want anyone else's hands on him. He clumsily removed her hands from his body and stepped back.

Carlos laughed. "Sorry ladies, he's happily taken. I suppose you'll have to make do with me tonight."

The girl in front of him pouted. "Aw come on, your girl doesn't need to know."

Rafe pushed past her and slumped into his seat at the bar. Fuck, he shouldn't have had that last shot; his head was spinning. He pulled out his phone and tried to open the Uber app. The persistent girl followed him to his seat and again tried to touch him, running her finger down his chest.

He growled and shoved her hand away roughly. "Hands off."

She huffed and removed her hand before pulling out her phone. "Well, if you're going to be like that, can you at least let me get a picture with you? My friends won't believe me without picture proof."

What is it with women in bars and fucking pictures? Fuck it, maybe if I get this over with, she'll finally leave me the fuck alone.

He stood, gripping the back of the barstool to steady himself as the room swam. The girl handed her phone to her friend, who was currently wrapped around Carlos like a damn octopus.

"Steph, quick! Take a picture for me!"

He started to turn toward the camera, when the girl's hands wrapped around his neck and *pulled*. He began to fall forward and she took advantage of his momentum, pressing her lips to his. He hardly noticed the flash of her camera phone as he put his hands on her shoulders and pushed her away.

"What the fuck?"

Carlos jumped up from his seat, pulling the girl away from him. "Not fucking cool, ladies. You better delete that goddamn picture. Come on, Rafe, let's get you home."

His friend slung Rafe's arm around his shoulder, taking his weight and walking them in the direction of the door. All Rafe could think about was getting to Sophie and kissing her. He needed to get the taste of that awful girl off of his lips.

Who the fuck does shit like this?

The air outside the bar was hot and humid, and Carlos had Rafe lean against the wall as he pulled out his phone and used his app to request a car. When the vehicle pulled up, Rafe slid into the front seat and gave the driver Sophie's address.

"Rafe, that's not how it works. I gave him the address to your apartment. You're fucking bombed, man; you need to go home."

He shook his head and repeated the address, leaning his head against the window. His head was still swimming, and he just wanted to lie down with Sophie wrapped in his arms.

He must've fallen asleep because when he next opened his eyes, they were in Sophie's driveway. Carlos opened the door and pulled Rafe out of the car, heading in the direction of the door. His head hit his chest, too heavy for him to hold up at this point.

Rafe heard a knock and the door opened. At the sound of Sophie's melodious voice, he smiled and lifted his head.

"Baby," he murmured.

"Jesus, Rafe. How fucking wasted are you?"

He tried to shrug but wasn't entirely sure the movement was successful. His body felt so heavy. "Had some shots."

Sophie laughed and gestured for Carlos to bring him into the house. When they made it into the bedroom, he fell back onto the bed. He heard Sophie and Carlos leave the room, and the sound of the front door closing before Sophie returned. She helped him strip down to his boxers, and he moved himself up to the pillow, grabbing Sophie's hand and pulling her down to join him. He wrapped his body around hers and kissed her shoulder.

"Love you, Soph," he muttered. He didn't hear her response, his eyelids finally drifting closed.

CHAPTER TWENTY-NINE

SOPHIE WOKE in the morning to the slight creak of her door opening. When she saw Kelsey in the doorway gesturing for her to come into the hallway, she gently removed herself from Rafe's embrace and walked out of her room. Kelsey pulled her into the living room, handing her a cup of coffee and gesturing for her to sit on the couch.

"I appreciate the coffee, but is there a reason you dragged me out of bed this early?"

The look in Kelsey's eyes made Sophie's heart pound. Her friend was looking at her with a mix of concern and anger. What had happened? She swore, if Kelsey's piece of shit ex-husband had hurt her again, she'd run him over with her car.

"Kels, what's going on? Did Kyle do something? Is James okay?"

"James is fine. He's with Kyle right now. I need to show you something." Kelsey took a deep breath, and Sophie's stomach dropped. "I was scrolling through pictures on

Instagram, looking up the 'Houston's Finest' hashtag and I came across pictures of Rafe and Carlos last night."

Sophie sighed. "You need to stop doing this to yourself. Every time you search that hashtag, you know you're going to find pictures of Carlos wrapped around some floozy."

Kelsey shook her head. "This isn't about Carlos, it's about Rafe. You need to see this picture."

Her friend handed Sophie her phone, and she could feel her hands shaking as she gripped the device. She didn't want to look down. Based on her friend's reaction alone, she knew what she would see, and she wasn't ready for the heartbreak it would bring. Kelsey nodded, confirming her suspicions, and Sophie took a deep breath, steeling herself before she looked down.

The picture was a bit blurry, clearly taken in a bar, and Sophie could feel her heart shattering as she took in the details. The image wasn't all that clear, but she could easily make out Rafe's broad shoulders and sandy blonde hair. He was leaning into a redhead, her arms around his neck and his lips on hers. Her breaths began to shorten, and she could feel the tears rolling down her cheeks.

How can this be happening to me again? Haven't I been cheated on enough?

Though she'd gone through this before, her former heartbreaks had nothing on this feeling. She felt as though she'd been stabbed, and she bent over, her hands on her stomach. Sophie was going to be sick, and she couldn't seem to suck in a full breath. She swore she could actually feel her heart shattering this time; the pain in her chest was real and all-consuming.

A high keening noise filled the room and she realized that it was coming from her. She barely felt Kelsey's arms wrap around her, and she couldn't make out any of the words her friend was uttering. Sophie didn't think she could come back from this one. How could she possibly recover? She had finally let herself fall for someone she thought was her future. They'd just professed their love for one another two nights ago. That night felt so far removed from this moment that she wondered if it had even happened in this lifetime.

Kelsey continued to rub her back, reminding her to breathe, encouraging her to suck in deep breaths and release them slowly. She wasn't sure how long she'd been sitting there before she heard his voice.

"Sophie? Baby, what's wrong?"

Kelsey released her and stood, but Sophie didn't turn around. She couldn't face him, couldn't look into his eyes without breaking down further.

Her friend's voice was filled with steel when she spoke. "You need to get the fuck out of our home. Now."

Rafe sputtered. "What are you talking about? What's going on? Sophie, baby, look at me. I don't understand what's happening."

"You piece of shit. There are pictures from last night, Rafe. Pictures of you kissing some other fucking woman," Kelsey spat.

Sophie remained hunched on the couch, still trying to get her breathing under control, the tears continuing to stream down her face.

"Last night? I don't—no." Rafe's voice broke on the last word. "Sophie, no. I was drunk and she kissed me. I pushed her away immediately. Please, you have to believe me. I would never cheat on you. Call Carlos, he saw the whole thing." His voice was desperate, and he sounded as though he was on the verge of tears himself.

She couldn't hold in the sounds anymore, and her sobs filled the room. She hardly recognized the noises leaving her mouth.

"Get the fuck out. NOW!" Kelsey yelled. "I will call the police if you don't leave in the next ten seconds."

"Okay, okay. I'll leave. Sophie, baby, I love you. I would never cheat on you. Please call me. I can explain everything."

Sophie didn't look up. She merely shook her head. She heard Rafe sigh and leave the room, the sound of the front door closing following his footsteps.

CHAPTER THIRTY

"FUCK!" Rafe's voice carried through his small apartment. He couldn't breathe and he didn't know what to do. His chest was tight, the anguish in Sophie's sobs echoing in his head, making him sick to his stomach. He needed to fix this, but he didn't know how. He only remembered pieces of last night, but he knew he'd pushed that girl away.

He pulled his phone from his pocket and called the only person who could help. Carlos didn't answer on the first call, so Rafe called repeatedly until he did.

"Fuck, it's eight in the morning and I'm hungover as hell. What is wrong with you, man?"

Rafe sucked in a breath and told Carlos about his morning, about waking up to find Sophie gone, his confrontation with Kelsey, and Sophie's reaction to the picture.

"You were there, man. You need to call Kelsey and tell her everything. I don't know what else to do. Sophie is everything to me, Carlos. Fucking everything."

"Alright, alright, calm down. I'll call Kelsey now. You

need to chill the fuck out though. Panicking isn't going to fix shit. We'll figure this out. I'll call you back in a few."

Rafe hung up the phone and paced his apartment. If this didn't work, he didn't know how to convince Sophie that it had all been a mistake. Why the hell had he gotten that drunk? If he'd taken fewer shots, or gone home sooner, none of this shit would've happened. He sat on the couch and put his head in his hands. The need to do something—anything—pulled at him. He couldn't just sit here while the only relationship that had ever meant something to him ended. He pulled at his hair in frustration.

Knowing he'd only drive himself crazy sitting here on the couch, he got up and headed to the bathroom. He smelled like a damn brewery, and all he wanted to do was wash the last twelve hours off of himself.

He'd just stepped out of the shower and wrapped a towel around his waist when he heard his phone ringing in the living room. He rushed to answer it, hoping against hope that it was Sophie. He just needed to hear her voice; he needed to hold her and tell her he loved her. They couldn't end like this—he wasn't ready for it, didn't know if he'd ever be ready for it.

He sighed when he saw the name on the screen, swiping to answer.

"Rafe? Okay, I called Kelsey. You better thank my ass because she fucking yelled at me for like ten minutes straight. I swear, my balls went into hiding, and I don't know if they'll ever come back out. That woman is goddamn terrifying."

"Carlos! What did she say?"

He sighed. "I think she believes me, but she said Sophie needs time. She wanted me to tell you to leave them alone."

"Fuck! Carlos, I can't just leave her alone. I need to talk to her, I need to explain."

"You need to give her space, dude. She knows the truth now. Let her think things through."

"Shit, you're right. Okay, I can do that. I can give her space. Thanks, man. I'll talk to you later."

Before he put his phone down, he texted Sophie.

Rafe: I'll give you time to think things through. Call me when you're ready to talk. I love you so much, Sophie. I'm not giving up on us. Take good care of our avocado for me.

CHAPTER THIRTY-ONE

SOPHIE WOKE up slowly on Monday morning, immediately reaching across the bed in search of Rafe's warmth. When her hand only felt cool, smooth sheets, she wrapped her arms around herself and let the tears come. She thought she'd be done crying by now, but the tears continued to come in waves, her grief hitting her again and again. She'd been cheated on—again. The thought alone stole the breath from her lungs.

Kelsey had told her all about Carlos's phone call yesterday, and Sophie wasn't sure it made a difference. If Carlos was to be believed, Rafe didn't actually cheat. Did that matter though? He'd put himself in that position: he'd chosen to get too drunk to function. And even if she was able to brush this aside and forgive him, would it change anything? Rafe would always have women behaving this way around him. Hell, the waitress on their first date had slipped him her damn number! She knew for a fact that women still called the paper trying to get his contact information, and she was sure women continued to throw themselves at him in his daily life.

Did she want to live like this? Always wondering if he would break and take one of those women up on their offer? She wanted to believe he would never cheat; he'd never given any indication that he would. She just wasn't sure she could overcome her own insecurities.

Sophie pulled herself out of bed and took a shower. Broken heart or not, she needed to get to work. Now that she wasn't being asked to write fluff pieces, she was happy with her role as a copyeditor. She still longed to edit novels, but had begun to wonder if she could offer her services to indie authors. The romance industry was beginning to lean more toward indie publishing, so she knew she would be able to find clients. If she built a name for herself, she may even be able to quit her job at the *Houston Reporter* and work as an editor only.

She'd been thinking about it more and more over the last few weeks. Working from home would give her time to raise her daughter, and with the way things had been progressing with Rafe, she wasn't sure she'd want to leave Houston.

Now though, Sophie wasn't sure what she wanted. She got ready quickly, tossing her hair into a messy bun and putting on a simple black T-shirt tucked into a flowy, floral-patterned skirt. It was one of the only skirts she currently owned that was comfortable over her baby bump. She smiled and ran her hand down her stomach.

"I'm not sure what's going to happen with your father, but at least I'll always have you."

She would pull herself together for her child. She needed to think about her daughter first, herself second. Sophie knew that Rafe would be in their life whether they worked out things between them or not, and she needed to stop wallowing and talk to him. She pulled out her phone and shot off a quick text.

Sophie: Can we talk tonight? I'll head over after work.

Rafe's response came within seconds, as though he'd been waiting to hear from her.

Rafe: Of course. I'll be here, Sophie.

She was getting ready to walk out the door when her phone rang in her hands. She didn't recognize the number, but it was from a New York area code.

"Hello?"

"Hi, is this Sophie Klein?"

"Yes," she replied hesitantly. She didn't recognize the man's voice and was anxious to see what the call was about.

"Great! My name is Chris, and I'm calling from Nottingham Publishing. Your boss, Karen, sent over a copy of your resume along with a fantastic letter of recommendation. She also sent me a portfolio of your work, and I have to say, I'm impressed. I would love to schedule a Skype interview with you today, if at all possible."

Sophie hadn't asked Karen about her recommendation letter in a few months, not sure that she even wanted it anymore with everything going on in her life. She should've known her boss would send it anyway. She'd never expected her dream job to come calling, and she wasn't quite sure how to react. Sophie didn't know that she would take the position, but she wanted to at least have options.

"Absolutely, I have free time at noon central standard time. Will that work for you?" she replied as calmly as possible. Internally, she was losing her shit, but she had at least managed to sound as though she had it together.

"Fantastic. I'll speak to you then, Sophie. I will send you a calendar invite with my Skype information."

"Thank you, Chris. I look forward to learning more about the position."

The interview went by in a blur, Sophie answering questions confidently and succinctly. She wasn't sure of much in her life right now, but she knew she was a damn good editor, and she was familiar with Nottingham Publishing and all of their imprints. She'd done her research. Chris was in his thirties, with brown hair, brown eyes, and a friendly smile that put her immediately at ease. Before long, they were just talking about their favorite upcoming releases, forgoing the formal interview entirely.

"Well, Sophie, I can say with a hundred percent certainty that you'd be an incredible fit for our team. How would you feel about relocating to New York?"

Sophie bit her lip. This was the part she wasn't sure about. She didn't know if she would be able to work things out with Rafe, but could she take their daughter away from him? He would be devastated if she moved to New York with their child.

"That's the part I'm not sure about, Chris. I'm pregnant, and the father of my child lives here in Houston."

"Well, I would really love to have you on our team. Editors can work remotely for the most part; let me see what I can work out with the higher-ups. Tell me this, though, would you be willing to travel to New York on a regular basis?"

Sophie contemplated it. Sure, it wasn't ideal, but Rafe or her father could watch their daughter while she was gone.

"I won't be able to travel in my third trimester, but after the baby is born, I'm sure I could work it out."

Chris nodded. "Okay, let me see what I can do. I'll let you know by the end of the week. I will ask that you consider a move to New York, however. Maybe the father would consider moving with you?"

Sophie swallowed. "I'll think about it. Thank you, Chris."

CHAPTER THIRTY-TWO

RAFE PACED HIS APARTMENT, running his hands through his hair nervously. Sophie was due to arrive any minute and he had no idea how this conversation would go. He hoped they could work it out; he couldn't imagine his life without her anymore. He'd been a complete mess for the last thirty-six hours. Hell, he had barely paid attention in his meeting with the sergeant this morning. He hoped he'd nodded in all of the right places, because he hadn't heard a word uttered. His heart stopped in his chest when he heard a knock at the door, and he took a deep breath before answering.

Fuck, she was gorgeous. There were bags under her eyes, and they were red-rimmed, as though she'd been crying, but she was still the most breathtaking woman he'd ever laid eyes on. He clenched his hands into fists, fighting the urge to reach for her and bury his head in her neck. He needed to hold her, but he knew she wasn't ready for that. Instead, Rafe stepped aside and gestured for her to come in. He should've probably said something, but his throat was clogged with emotion, and he was so damn nervous.

Sophie sat on the couch and looked over at him. He studied her face, trying to read her thoughts, desperate to figure out how she was feeling. He joined her on the couch, sitting on the opposite end to avoid making her feel uncomfortable.

Sophie cleared her throat, her hands in her lap. She fidgeted with the material of her floral-patterned skirt for a few moments before speaking.

"I believe you," she said quietly.

The air whooshed out of Rafe's lungs in one long breath. "Thank fuck, Sophie. I would never cheat on you. Never. You're it for me." He reached for her hand, and she pulled it away gently. Confused, he met her gaze. There were tears in her beautiful green eyes, and he knew things were about to go downhill quickly.

"I believe you, but that doesn't change anything, Rafe. You'll always get female attention, and with my past, I just don't know that I can handle it. I don't want to constantly worry about you, about this. I just don't think that I can be with you."

Rafe's chest constricted and he lowered his head into his hands. Fuck, she believed him and it still wasn't enough. She was still fucking leaving him.

"Sophie, you know I don't want the attention. I don't give two shits about the vapid women who fucking throw themselves at me because I'm a police officer, or because I look like a fucking stripper. You're the only person whose opinion matters to me."

Sophie was crying in earnest now, and he couldn't fight the urge to comfort her anymore. Moving to her side of the couch, he took hold of her chin, tilting her face up so that he could wipe the tears from her cheeks. He kissed her lightly on the lips, trying to convey how he felt without words.

Sophie groaned and sunk into him, her tongue sweeping into his mouth. Her sweet taste filled his mouth and his heart soared. Nothing in his life had ever tasted better, had ever felt so fucking right. He moved his hands down her body, skimming past her breasts, his hands molding to the curve of her hips. He lifted her and pulled her into his lap, Sophie's legs straddling his own. He thrust up, his hardening cock needing the contact. He was desperate for her, fucking ravenous. He needed to show her that she was all he'd ever want or need.

Rafe's hands slipped up her thigh, and Sophie pulled away roughly, scrambling off his lap and stepping back. Her chest was heaving, her breaths coming rapidly.

"No, Rafe. I told you I can't fucking do this." She choked on a sob. "Do you have any idea what it felt like to see that picture of you kissing another woman? It was easily the worst moment of my life. I can't—" Sophie gasped for breath, doubling over and wrapping her arms around herself.

When she had gained control of her breathing and looked up at him, her eyes were hard, resolved. "I can't go through that again, Rafe. I *won't*."

Rafe didn't know what to do or say. Her pain was palpable; he could feel it like it was his own, and something in him broke. He pulled at his hair, struggling to think of a way to change her mind. "Fuck! I don't know what to do, Sophie. Tell me how to fix this and I'll do it. I need to fix it, please."

She shook her head and took another step back, tears still flowing freely. "There's nothing, Rafe. We can't be fixed." She took a deep breath and wiped the tears from her eyes.

"I got a job offer in New York today, and I'm considering it. I know it would complicate things with custody, but it's my dream job. I haven't made a decision yet, but I wanted you to know."

Rafe jerked back, feeling as though he'd been slapped. A life without his baby? A life without Sophie? He felt the family he'd always wanted slipping through his fingers. Panic clawed its way up his throat, making his voice hoarse when he spoke.

"Sophie, please," his voice broke, and he got down on his knees in front of her. "Please don't take her away from me. I need you two, please don't go. Don't do this."

He leaned forward, resting his head on her stomach. "This—you and our daughter—is all I've ever wanted. If you leave—"

Rafe stopped, unable to finish the sentence, but knowing that Sophie leaving would fucking destroy him.

"I don't know yet, Rafe. I haven't made the decision. I don't want to take your daughter away from you, but I don't want to turn down my dream job either."

He stood, pacing the apartment once more, thinking through his options. He'd just been offered the detective position, but he hadn't signed the paperwork yet. He could give up his dream job so that she could pursue hers, right? Fuck, he needed time to work this out, to come up with a plan.

Sophie stood from her spot on the couch. "I should go. Kelsey and I are having a girls' night. I need to think things through, but I'll call you."

Rafe nodded and walked toward her. He placed one hand on her cheek, looking into her eyes, begging her to pay attention to the love there. "What about us, Sophie? Are you still thinking things through?"

"No, Rafe. I told you. I can't do this with you. We can be co-parents, but I can't be in a relationship that I'm not secure in."

Without another word, Sophie pulled away from his grasp and turned, walking out the door and taking his baby with her. The sound of the lock engaging filled his apartment, and Rafe sunk to the floor, feeling as though he'd lost everything he'd ever wanted.

CHAPTER THIRTY-THREE

EIGHTEEN WEEKS PREGNANT

THE NEXT WEEK of Sophie's life passed in a blur. She went to work, came home, ate her feelings, and cried herself to sleep alone in her bed. Never had a breakup hit her this hard. In the past she'd been sad, sure, but more angry than anything. Without Rafe though, all she felt was a crippling despair. More and more, she began to doubt her choices. Hadn't Rafe proven at every given opportunity that he wasn't like her exes?

Throughout their entire relationship, he'd been sweet and attentive, never making her feel second to anyone else, his eyes never straying in public. She knew deep down that he'd never actually cheat. Honestly, that knowledge was what made the entire situation so difficult. Sophie knew without a doubt that the issue was her own. Her past relationships had destroyed her confidence, making her doubt not only herself but the men she chose to let into her life.

Her fear was debilitating, and painful. Not only was she hurting herself, she was hurting Rafe—something she never wanted to do. Maybe down the road they could try to be together, once she'd grappled with her own demons and worked past her issues. With that goal in mind, she made an appointment with a therapist, determined to sort herself out. Her first session was the following day and she was feeling pretty hopeful about it.

In the meantime, she'd made a decision and needed to speak to her boss about it. Sophie took a deep breath, smoothed her dress over her baby bump, and walked to her boss's office. The door was partially open, so Sophie knocked gently before entering. Karen was on the phone and smiled at Sophie while holding up her finger to indicate she needed a minute.

Sophie took a seat in front of Karen's desk, running through her proposal in her head. She wasn't sure what Karen would say about her idea, but she needed to at least try. All too soon, Karen hung up the phone and gave Sophie her full attention.

"I presume you're here to turn in your two weeks' notice? Sources tell me you've been offered a job in New York?"

Sophie cleared her throat, giving herself one more moment to gather her thoughts. "Actually, Karen, as much as I appreciate your help, I'm turning down the offer in New York. I'd love to live there, but I want to raise my child here, with family. Which brings me to my reason for being here. I would like to ask if it's possible for me to copyedit only, and remotely. I'd like to start offering my editing services to indie authors and would need to be home to get that business off the ground. There are a lot of great authors out there who need freelance editors, and I would like to be that for them. Until I build a solid client base, though, I need to have a reliable source of income. Which is where, uh, you come in."

Sophie snapped her mouth shut before she could

continue to ramble. Deciding to stay in Houston had been easier than she'd thought. The job in New York had been a dream of hers for as long as she could remember, but she wanted to raise her child near her father and Rafe. A move would be selfish, and really, she could be an amazing editor anywhere. The indie market was only growing; now was the ideal time to start a freelance business. She really could have it all—her family nearby and a job she loved.

Unfortunately, Karen—a huge deciding factor in her new career path—had fallen completely silent. Her boss's expression was difficult to read, but she looked as though she were trying to read Sophie's thoughts. Her gaze was penetrating and just when Sophie was about to break and speak, Karen nodded, coming to a decision.

"You're a damn good copyeditor, Sophie. I'd be stupid not to keep you on in some capacity. I can't let you work completely remotely though. I would need you to come to the staff meeting once per week, and you will continue to have an office here. After the weekly meeting, I expect you to maintain four hours of office time. That way, our journalists and the rest of our team have access to you. Does that work?"

Sophie could hardly believe it. She had honestly expected a downright refusal, or at least for Karen to be upset that Sophie had wasted her coveted recommendation. After a moment, she realized that Karen was waiting for her to speak.

"Yes! That's fantastic! Thank you so much, Karen!"

Karen shrugged, as though the offer was no big deal. "Hey, it's a better option than losing one of my best editors. I think you'll do great things, Sophie, and I'm honestly happy to hear that you're staying. Now get out of my office; I have work to get done."

Sophie laughed and left the office quickly. For the first time in a week, she had a genuine smile on her face. She may not have Rafe, but she had a plan for her life and for her baby. Things were starting to look up. It was only when she returned to her office and picked up her phone to call someone with the good news that the sadness returned. Her thumb hovered over Rafe's name for a brief moment before moving down and selecting Kelsey's. She was moving forward, but she still wasn't ready to reach out to Rafe. She had more work to do first.

A month later, Sophie had successfully transitioned into working from home, setting up a small work area in the living room of the house she shared with Kelsey and James. She'd seen her new therapist weekly and was starting to feel better about herself. Sophie was beginning to realize that her trust issues ultimately stemmed from her relationship with her mother. It had been a hard truth to accept, and many tears had been shed that session, but she felt lighter afterwards.

At twenty-one weeks pregnant, her baby was now the size of a bok choy and was hungry enough that she ate pretty much constantly. Keeping Rafe in mind, she made sure all of her meals and snacks were healthy and full of protein. Though she still hadn't spoken to Rafe on the phone or seen him, he checked in with her every few days, always asking about the baby's health. He hadn't tried to push her into talking to him or seeing him, for which she was grateful. She knew that the moment she saw him, she would need to be in his arms, feel his solid, comforting warmth surrounding her. She was making progress with herself, but she wasn't quite ready yet.

She had told Rafe almost immediately that she'd turned down the job in New York, but she had yet to tell him about the business she was starting. His response to the news that she was staying in Houston had seemed subdued, but she knew that it was only because he was trying not to push her or get her hopes up. He really was such an incredible man, and she hoped that she could earn his forgiveness. The time apart was hard for her too, but she wanted to be sure that she was ready to handle a commitment without bolting again.

The ping of her phone interrupted her thoughts and she picked it up to read the text from Karen.

Karen: A letter to the editor just came across my desk. Thought you'd like to read it before it gets printed tomorrow. I've emailed it to you.

Sophie felt her brows knit in confusion. Letters to the editor didn't need to be copyedited; they were usually printed as is. It was part of what made them so charming and sometimes humorous. She pulled up the tab on her laptop that contained her work email and clicked on her most recent message from Karen. What she saw there took her breath away.

Dear Editor,

First of all, thank you and your staff for the incredible series of features you wrote about me and my partner, Carlos. The reporter who shared our story did an incredible job. To be honest, she's actually the reason I'm writing this letter.

You see, editor, I'm in love with her. Not the kind of love you see in the movies, not that Hollywood contrived version of it. Real, deep, meaningful love. The kind of love that changes a man.

Before that reporter, I had a hard time opening up, so sure that my past would lead to judgment and ridicule. She taught me that my past isn't something to be ashamed of because it made me the man I am today. So here it is—the unedited, gory truth of my childhood.

I was orphaned at a young age, my mother overdosing on heroin right in front of me. Due to years of abuse and neglect, I was half starved and didn't even know my own name. I named myself after a Ninja Turtle, actually, because I looked up to them.

I spent years in and out of foster care, sure that I would never find a family to love. Then, a nosy, frustrating, beautiful woman came into my life, and she somehow managed to give me everything I'd ever wanted.

Now I'm sure you're wondering what the point of this letter is. I'm writing this letter to you as a declaration. Women of

Houston: as flattering as the attention has been, I am as off the market as a man can be. Even though I've messed things up with my favorite reporter, I plan to spend the rest of my life winning her back. So, please, I beg you, if you see me on the street or on patrol, keep your hands and phone numbers to yourselves. Instead, feel free to give all of your attention to my ridiculous excuse for a partner, Carlos.

I only have eyes for one woman, and nothing anyone says or does will ever change that.

Yours Truly,
Rafe Pierce, Formerly 'Houston's Hot Cop'

Sophie read Rafe's letter three times. It was absolutely perfect, a declaration of love and loyalty that she never imagined she would get or deserve. In that moment, all of her carefully laid plans and all of her fears flew out the window. She didn't want to spend another minute away from Rafe. Already piecing an idea together, Sophie picked up her phone and scrolled through her contacts. There was only one person in her life crazy enough to help her with what she wanted to do.

CHAPTER THIRTY-FOUR

ONE WHOLE MONTH. That's how long it had been since Rafe had last laid eyes on Sophie. Each moment was excruciating. He missed her so much that, at times, it was hard to breathe. At random moments throughout his day, he would find himself clutching his chest as though in physical pain. He'd like to say that he'd held it together these past weeks, but he hadn't.

The entire first week of their separation had been a drunk blur. He'd become closely acquainted with a few very fine bottles of Scotch. It wasn't until Carlos had slapped sense into him, literally, that Rafe had stopped wallowing and formulated a plan. The first thing he'd done was turn down the detective position. If Sophie wanted to move to New York, he would follow her. She'd told him that she'd turned down the position, but Rafe wanted her to know she had options. He could work his way up through the ranks again, but he would never find another Sophie.

Then, he'd waited, waited for Sophie to come to him. It took all of his self-restraint to only text her every few days to check in. It wasn't just Sophie he missed, of course. He missed talking to his baby, feeling her kick, contemplating names for her with Sophie. Finally, he'd decided to make his move. It had been risky, writing to her newspaper and exposing his past and his emotions to the entire city. He was sure to get made fun of endlessly at work, but it would all be worth it if his declaration made Sophie feel confident in him, in them.

He'd meant what he'd said in that letter too: he would never give up. He would spend his whole damn life fighting for Sophie. Of course, his dick was not pleased with this decision, and he was ashamed to admit he'd practically rubbed himself raw over the course of the last few weeks. Carlos had, naturally, suggested that he go to a bar for a random hookup. Rafe had responded with a sound punch to his friend's jaw. Carlos had changed the subject quickly.

Rafe heard Carlos's phone vibrate and looked over to see his partner grinning like a fool. Rafe scowled in return; he was not in the mood to hear about another of Carlos's endless hookups.

"Hey man, we need to make a quick stop."

"I'm hungry as hell, and you're the one who dragged me out of the house to eat in the first place. You better not be using me for a ride to a fucking booty call."

Carlos sighed. "I won't lie, a hot lay would be nice right now. But that isn't what this is about."

Instead of giving Rafe an address to punch into his GPS, his partner gave him directions. Before long, Rafe began to recognize their surroundings and shot a confused look at Carlos.

"The courthouse? Why are we going to the courthouse, Carlos?"

His friend sighed. "Can't you just let this be a fucking surprise? You're so damn high maintenance."

Rafe barked out a laugh and parked his car in the metered parking lot across the street from the courthouse. "Alright, lead the way then."

Carlos led them into the building and up to the second floor. When they reached an office bearing a name he didn't recognize, Rafe shot his friend a puzzled look.

"This is your stop. I think you'll want to walk through that door."

Rafe scowled. "Unless there's food in there, I'm going to murder you. I was promised a meal and you brought me to a damn courthouse with absolutely no explanation."

Carlos scoffed. "I'm sorry, princess, do you need a Snickers? Should I start calling you Officer Hangry instead of Officer Pencil Dick? Just walk through the door, jackass. You'll like what you find, even if it isn't edible."

Heaving a heavy sigh, Rafe twisted the doorknob and entered the room. His heart stopped in his chest at the sight before him. Though he'd been trained for years to take in all of his surroundings when entering an unfamiliar room, he saw nothing but Sophie. She was smiling brightly at him, wearing a white sundress that barely concealed her still-growing stomach. Her hair fell in loose waves down her back, and she was without a doubt, the most beautiful sight he'd ever beheld.

"Sophie," he breathed her name. He wanted to cross the room and take her into his arms, but he was worried this was all an illusion. He shook his head. "What are we doing here?"

Sophie crossed the room slowly, her smile soft and warm. Rafe's heart thundered in his chest at her proximity, his fingers itching to find her hips.

"Rafe, I read the letter you wrote to the editor. First of all, let me apologize for ever doubting you."

"Sophie, you don't have to—"

She covered his mouth with her hand, effectively silencing him. "I do have to, Rafe. I've been working with a therapist for a few weeks now. I'm trying to sort through my trust issues and I've realized that I reacted too harshly. Every man I've ever been with hurt me, and if possible, I love you more than I loved all of them combined. Honestly, knowing how I feel about you makes me doubt that I ever loved any of them. I wanted to work on myself before talking to you about us, but I've realized that I want to work on my issues with you. I don't think I can spend another moment without you. I've been…" Sophie's breath hitched and tears filled her eyes. Reflexively, he reached up to wipe them away. Sophie placed her hand over his on her cheek, holding it there.

"I've been miserable without you. You're my other half, Rafe. Which is why I'm asking you here, in this dingy courthouse…" She laughed and took a deep breath. "To marry me."

Rafe's eyes traced every inch of Sophie's face, taking in the faint blush tingling her cheeks, the sweet curve of her lips, and the hope in her eyes. She was a dream come true and he couldn't believe she even had to ask.

"Carlos managed to pull some strings, and all you have to do is sign the marriage certificate. He also used the spare key you gave me to grab a suit from your apartment. It's waiting for you in the bathroom if you say yes. We can get married right here, right now. That is, if you want to."

Forcing his gaze from Sophie with some effort, he took in his surroundings. He was in a small office and there, on the desk, was a marriage certificate. He approached the desk slowly, still not fully trusting that this was actually happening. He ran his hands down the piece of paper, his fingers tracing the loops and swirls of Sophie's signature. This was *real*, and it was everything he could've hoped for.

He must've lingered on the document for longer than he'd thought, because Sophie broke the silence of the room with a nervous ramble.

"This was a terrible idea, wasn't it? Of course you don't want to marry me. I just admitted I had issues—who would want to deal with that?"

He shook his head and turned to face her. He cupped her cheek with one hand, using the fingertips of the other to trace the familiar features of her face. "Sophie, I'd marry you in a trash dump if it meant spending my life with you. Everyone has issues, babe. Look at Carlos—the man has more problems than the Kardashians."

A pointed cough and a muttered "jackass" was audible through the closed door, letting Rafe know that his friend was listening in on the conversation. He held back his chuckle and continued.

"What makes a marriage work is the ability to work on issues *together*. I'm far from perfect, and I'm sure you and I will have plenty of struggles in our long life together, but if we keep the lines of communication open and support each other, we will be just fine. However, I'm a little bummed I won't get to plan some epic proposal. I mean, let's face it, I am the romantic in this relationship."

Sophie's smile was blinding. "Open and honest communication, huh? I can definitely do that. Now hurry up and kiss me, big guy. We have a ceremony to get to."

HOUSTON'S FINEST COUPLE

As stated in his letter to the editor, Rafe Pierce is officially off the market. One half of Houston's Finest was married on a quiet Tuesday afternoon in a small, no-fuss courthouse ceremony. The bride wore a simple, white sundress and a radiant smile as she said her vows, and rumor has it, the best man cried at the couple's heartfelt impromptu words. Congratulations to our very own Sophie Klein on her nuptials—we are beyond thrilled for the happy couple.

EPILOGUE

"MR. AND MRS. PIERCE, meet your beautiful daughter. She's twenty-one and a half inches, and seven and a half pounds."

Sophie swallowed the lump in her throat as the nurse placed her child into her arms for the very first time. Even covered in goop, she was the most breathtaking sight Sophie had ever beheld. She reached over and grabbed Rafe's hand, looking away from their baby briefly to meet his eyes. He looked every inch as in love with their daughter as she was. His smile lightened his entire face as his eyes flicked from her face to their baby's. He leaned down to place a small kiss on the top of her head before reaching a finger out to run along their daughter's small cheek.

"We have to take her away for a moment to clean her up. Have you thought of a name yet?"

Sophie smiled. "Yes, her name is Donatella Kady Pierce. Ella for short."

Rafe grinned back. "Now we have two Ninja Turtles in

the family. I need you to pop out two boys for me, babe. We need the whole bunch."

The nurse took Ella from her arms to clean and wrap her up, and Sophie rolled her eyes. "If you think I'm doing that again anytime soon, you're crazy. You remember all of the screaming, right? Those weren't exactly painless screams, Rafe."

Rafe hummed and kissed her softly. "I guess I'll just have to start seducing the hell out of you in six weeks when you're cleared for sex."

Her husband's eyes gleamed wickedly and Sophie felt herself blush, hoping none of the nurses had heard his lewd comment. She imagined he wouldn't have to try very hard to seduce her. The man was fucking irresistible.

A few hours later, Rafe and Sophie were in their recovery room resting when they heard a light knock on the door. The baby was sleeping, so Rafe stood up to let their visitors in. He held a finger to his mouth to indicate Kelsey and Becky needed to be quiet as they entered. The pair stopped to quickly hug Sophie before making their way to the small crib Ella slept in. They cooed quietly, telling Sophie and Rafe how beautiful their daughter was.

Another light knock startled them from their gushing, and Rafe walked to the door once again to let in another visitor. An unfamiliar nurse entered the room, smiling at Sophie briefly before turning to Rafe.

"Mr. Pierce?" she asked.

"Yes, that's me," he responded slowly, clearly not sure what was going on.

The nurse wrung her hands in front of her, looking down for a moment before meeting Rafe's gaze. "I'm afraid I have some bad news for you, sir. I'm so sorry to barge in on you right now, but you were listed as the emergency contact for Carlos Ramirez. We were unable to reach you when we tried to call, but one of the nurses recognized your name and directed me to this floor."

Dread filled Sophie's gut and she heard a sharp breath pass through Kelsey's lips. They all knew that what the nurse was about to say would be devastating. Rafe waved the nurse on, and Sophie saw him swallow, clearly too worried to speak.

"I'm afraid there has been an accident, Mr. Pierce."

Kelsey rushed across the room, forgetting to lower her voice in her panic. "What kind of accident. Where is Carlos?"

"He's in intensive care at the moment. He was t-boned by a drunk driver. Fortunately, he was only a few blocks from the hospital, but there was some swelling in his brain, and he hasn't regained consciousness yet."

The sound of a stifled sob pulled her gaze from the nurse and she looked for the source. Sophie watched a wide variety of emotions flicker across her friend's face, ranging from disbelief to overwhelming sadness. Kelsey covered her mouth with a shaking hand, and Becky moved across the room to wrap an arm around her silently shaking shoulders.

"Is..." Rafe took a steadying breath, his fists clenching at his sides. It was clear he was trying to hold himself together. "Is he going to wake up though? You said *yet*; that means he will wake up, right?"

"We're hopeful that he will recover, yes. However, we still don't know what kind of brain damage he suffered. We won't know until he comes to. I'm so sorry to be the bearer of bad news on a day like today. I'll be waiting in the hall. Let me know when you're ready to go down and see him."

The nurse left the room, shutting the door silently behind her. Rafe walked to Sophie's bed and leaned his forehead against hers, as though he needed to borrow her strength for what was to come next. His breaths were ragged, and it wasn't until he wiped away her tears that she realized she was crying as well.

They stayed in the same position for what felt like an eternity, Rafe clearly working to regain his composure while Kelsey's sobs filled the quiet room.

COMING NEXT

Now that Rafe & Sophie got their happily ever after, stay tuned for the next book in the Houston's Finest Series, *Needing to Love You* featuring Carlos and Kelsey!

COMING SPRING 2019!

Erin Rylie is a Montana born, Texas raised New Jersey transplant with a degree in hospitality. At 29 years old, she decided it was finally time for to pursue her real passion in life—writing! She's been writing princess stories and LOTR fan-fiction since she was in middle school, so the transition into romance has been fun!

When she's not writing, she's reading (fantasy, sci-fi and romance are her favorite genres) or working. She's currently obsessed with Brooklyn Nine Nine, which should tell you all you need to know about her sense of humor.

Finally, she is 100% an old cat lady. Her cats, Socks and Kaz are little weirdos and she loves them more than most people.

Find my website at www.erinryliewrites.com

- facebook.com/erinryliewrites
- instagram.com/erinryliewrites
- goodreads.com/erinrylie

ACKNOWLEDGMENTS

I'll be completely honest, an acknowledgments page isn't something I ever expected to be writing. Publishing a book has been a dream of mine since I was a nerdy little middle-schooler, writing *Lord of the Rings* fan fiction in the basement of my mom's house. If this gets a little long-winded, I apologize in advance! There are just so many people who made this possible for me.

First of all, thank you to everyone who has taken the time to read *Hating to Love You*. Rafe popped into my head one day after reading a newspaper article about "Michigan's Hot Cop," and I'm so happy that I got to share his story. He and Sophie both mean a lot to me, and I hope that they won you over as well.

A HUGE thanks go out to my Dad, Mom, and Hermine. When I told you three that I wanted to quit the career I'd built for myself to move to NY and try writing a book, none of you batted an eyelash, you just helped me plan my move. I love you all so much for your support.

Kelsey, my bestie, my parabati—I genuinely can't thank

you enough for your help. Thank you for taking every single one of my late-night phone calls, for Facetiming me when I got stuck and needed help plotting, for waking me up from naps with the most ridiculous string of texts you could think of, and for encouraging me to finish a book I never imagined I would be able to write. Thank you for reading the first draft of this book and every draft since. Thank you for being such an incredible friend.

To my editor, Erica—you have gone above and beyond what I imagined an editor would do. Believing in my writing has helped me get through my first editing process and you've encouraged me to keep writing. Because of you, I honestly believe I can make a career out of this.

Brooke, our friendship has meant more to me than you could possibly know. You've been my mentor and my shoulder to cry on. I am eternally grateful that our random IG messaging turned into such an amazing friendship. Thank you for helping me through the self-publishing process and for editing every one of my teasers for me. Your font obsession absolutely comes in handy!

To Amélie, the little sister I've always wanted. I can't wait for you to grow up and read this book. Yes, you will be a reader—I'm determined. I love you more than you could possibly imagine, and I can't wait to watch you grow up. Always remember, you can do anything you set your mind to.

Finally, thank you to my Instagram followers for supporting me through this CRAZY journey.

Made in the USA
Middletown, DE
05 January 2019